▶ Erotic Memoirs and Postfeminism

DOI: 10.1057/9781137326546

Other Palgrave Pivot titles

DOI: 10.1057/9781137326546

palgrave▶**pivot**

Erotic Memoirs and Postfeminism: The Politics of Pleasure

Joel Gwynne

National Institute of Education, Singapore

palgrave
macmillan

DOI: 10.1057/9781137326546

First published 2013 by
PALGRAVE MACMILLAN

Palgrave Macmillan in the UK is an imprint of Macmillan Publishers Limited, registered in England, company number 785998, of Houndmills, Basingstoke, Hampshire RG21 6XS.

Palgrave Macmillan in the US is a division of St Martin's Press LLC, 175 Fifth Avenue, New York, NY 10010.

Palgrave Macmillan is the global academic imprint of the above companies and has companies and representatives throughout the world.

Palgrave® and Macmillan® are registered trademarks in the United States, the United Kingdom, Europe and other countries.

ISBN: 978–1–137–32655–3 EPUB
ISBN: 978–1–137–32654–6 PDF
ISBN: 978–1–137–32653–9 Hardback

A catalogue record for this book is available from the British Library.

A catalog record for this book is available from the Library of Congress.

www.palgrave.com/pivot

DOI: 10.1057/9781137326546

For Zulaihah and the boy.

DOI: 10.1057/9781137326546

Contents

DOI: 10.1057/9781137326546

Introduction

Abstract: *By mapping the theoretical and cultural framework surrounding the publishing phenomena of contemporary women's erotic memoirs, and by illustrating the genre's status as a subdivision of chick lit, this chapter locates the scope and aims of this study as one which analyses the relationship between erotic memoirs and the politics of third-wave feminism and postfeminism as a cultural condition.*

▶ Gwynne, Joel. *Erotic Memoirs and Postfeminism: The Politics of Pleasure.* Basingstoke: Palgrave Macmillan, 2013. DOI: 10.1057/9781137326546.

In a statement that could be read as deceptively simple, Joseph Bristow comments that sexuality has emerged as a term that "points to both internal and external phenomena, to both the realm of the psyche and the material world".[1] Bristow's words gesture towards a conceptualisation of sexuality as a blank canvas upon which we inscribe a plurality of meanings and identities. Precisely for this reason, our understanding of sexuality is a project never completed, commensurate with the manner in which sexual identities evolve in accordance to the movements of culture. The tripartite relationship between our personal experience of sexuality, our conceptualisation of sexuality, and our culture's attitudes towards sexuality, is complex. Jeffrey Weeks has observed that "what we believe sexuality is, or ought to be, structures our responses to it", and hence it is difficult to separate the "particular meanings we give to sex from the forms of control we advocate".[2] Historically, societies have responded to the complexity of sexuality by reductively positioning erotic activity as a socially polarised force, as either "dangerous, disruptive and fundamentally antisocial" or "benign, life-enhancing and liberating".[3] Weeks defines the "absolutist" position as one adhering to the former conceptualisation of sexuality, a moral and political framework that proposes authoritarian regulation, while the "libertarian" position is likely to propose a "relaxed, even radical set of values".[4] Recognising the simplicity of this binary interpretive model, Weeks offers a third way of understanding human sexuality – the "liberal-pluralist" position – oriented around an awareness of the perils of both moral authoritarianism and sexual excess.

Arguing that these three "strategies of regulation" still provide the framework – whether consciously or not – for current debates about sex and politics, Weeks contends that it is the absolutist tradition that remains dominant and is based on intransigent beliefs that the "disruptive powers of sex can only be controlled by a clear-cut morality, intricately embedded in a particular set of social institutions: marriage, heterosexuality, family life".[5] Gayle Rubin argues persuasively that sexual activity outside of these socially sanctioned "safe zones" is treated with suspicion and condemnation, concomitant with the manner in which Western culture "construes and judges any sexual practice in terms of its worst possible expression".[6] The absolutist tradition is founded on theorisations that are biologically essentialist, and in response much of contemporary sexological research has been concerned with demonstrating how sexuality possesses no intrinsic meaning but rather embodies the imprint of a

DOI: 10.1057/9781137326546

vast range of social meanings, encouraging us to accept that the "value systems built around [sexuality] have to be understood as both historical and contingent".[7] Rosalind Coward has illustrated the importance of understanding how historical moments not only shape our attitudes to sexuality, but also present opportunities for "a massive relearning" about sexual identity. Employing the moral panic surrounding AIDS in the 1980s as an example – a period "where penetration might literally spell death" – Coward suggests that the historical moment served to create a female space where "sexuality could be redefined as something other than male discharge into any kind of receptacle".[8]

The perspectives of Weeks and Coward demonstrate how sexuality and feminist studies often converge, for both are committed to positioning sexuality as a social construct. Yet, it is important to bear in mind that, broadly speaking, sexuality studies are oriented around critical analyses of the existing organisation and social meaning of sex – most particularly sexual object choice and desire – while feminist studies is committed to analysing the relationship between gender and sexed identities. Chris Beasley argues that sexuality studies has predominantly theorised male sexuality and the experiences of gay men, a focus that occurred "partly because of a residual traditional privileging of men's perspectives and partly because lesbians have sometimes seen themselves, and have been seen, in relation to women's experiences".[9] Concurrent with contemporary trends in sexological constructionist research, the chapters in this book seek to position sexuality as a fictional unity of disparate bodily and mental processes, identities as historically constituted, gender as a social imperative rather than a biological given, and the erotic as inseparable from social relations of institutional power and domination. Yet, the distinction between sexuality studies and feminist studies is an important one to make, for while the following chapters locate popular erotic memoirs in the context of sexuality studies, they do so through examining the place of contemporary female sexuality within theoretical debates surrounding contemporary feminism, most notably third-wave feminism and postfeminism as a cultural condition.

The analysis of memoirs within this book builds on debates that have raged over the last 20 years, however it is important to briefly emphasize that the discussion of sexuality was, of course, also central to second-wave feminism. In *Is the Future Female? Troubled Thoughts on Contemporary Feminism* (1987), Lynne Segal decrees that the politicisation of sexuality fostered by the ascent of second-wave feminism was

DOI: 10.1057/9781137326546

central to the movement's counterculture, for movement feminists were not only anti-patriarchy but also anti-imperialist and anti-authoritarian. Sexual empowerment was, therefore, mobilised as paramount in a revolution against a capitalist bureaucracy that required sexually repressed individuals "for the realization of its life-negating, endlessly acquisitive, and destructive goals", a mode of social organisation contingent upon "self-restraint and compulsive work", both antithetical to "liberated or spontaneous sexual expression".[10] Deconstructing essentialist histories of sexuality was imperative to the endeavour of deconstructing patriarchal capitalist ideologies, as was reappraising the sources of women's sexual pleasure by specifically underscoring the relationship between suppressed sexuality and social powerlessness. For many second-wave feminists, social powerlessness was constituted not merely by the subjugation of female sexual desire, but through the responsibility of acting as "moral custodians of male [sexual] behaviour", which women themselves were (and still are) perceived as "instigating and eliciting".[11] More discursively, feminists challenged the host of sanctions and constraints – legal, social and ideological – that permeate every aspect of women's sexuality, driven by the recognition that "men's greater power in the world is manifested in, and often mediated through, sexual encounters".[12]

Speaking for not only herself but for movement feminists more expansively, Lynne Segal recollects, "our sexual conquests – for that is how we saw them – were most satisfying for the social status they conferred on us rather than the physical pleasure they provided."[13] This confession is important for not only its declaration of the political intentions of active female sexuality, but also in its recognition that this form of political subversion did little to reconfigure tactile experiences of female sexual pleasure. Pursuing the cultural aftershock of second-wave interventions, *Erotic Memoirs and Postfeminism* seeks to explore the manner in which postfeminism and third-wave feminism have emerged – concurrently with the development of neo-liberalism as a global system of governance – as movements and cultural conditions which centralise female sexuality. Prior to embarking upon Chapter 1's more extended discussion of postfeminism, it is important to briefly contextualise and clarify the terms associated with new feminisms, shrouded as they are in contention and contrariness.

Sarah Projansky defines postfeminism as both a "self-defined particular historical moment" and a "versatile cultural discourse, one that negotiates, defines, and ultimately limits what feminism is within popular

DOI: 10.1057/9781137326546

culture".[14] For Projansky, postfeminism is indicative of the "pervasiveness of the assumption in popular culture that feminism existed, was wholeheartedly absorbed by the mainstream, and therefore is no longer needed".[15] Stéphanie Genz and Benjamin Brabon further highlight the complexities of the term, suggesting that postfeminism has "confounded and split contemporary critics with its contradictory meanings and pluralistic outlook",[16] representing not merely a "conceptual and semantic bond with feminism but also relations with other social, cultural, theoretical and political areas",[17] such as consumer culture, popular media and neo-liberal rhetoric. While Genz and Brabon advocate an interrogation of the term that is attentive to the liberating possibilities of postfeminist culture, critics such as Angela McRobbie have remained sceptical, arguing that postfeminism is "a process by which feminist gains of the 1970s and 1980s are actively and relentlessly undermined", proposing that through "an array of machinations, elements of contemporary popular culture are perniciously effective in regard to this undoing of feminism, while simultaneously appearing to be engaging in a well-informed and even well-intended response to feminism".[18]

Perhaps due to their cohabitation along a similar historical and theoretical trajectory, postfeminism and third-wave feminism are often positioned as related, if not imbricated concepts. Yet, in the context of femininity, Genz and Brabon clarify that the distinction between "girl" and "grrrl" may be used to "illustrate a common perception of a much wider division between postfeminism and third-wave feminism, whereby the former is interpreted as middle-of-the-road and depoliticised while the latter is more subcultural and activist".[19] While postfeminism is marked by its "acceptance, use and manipulation of its insider position within popular culture",[20] third-wave feminist writing has been largely the product of women under 40 who interrogate and deconstruct popular culture, and whose work is conceived and articulated outside of mainstream cultural praxis. In opposition to postfeminist declarations of women's achievement and equality in the wider social world, third-wave feminists see the "war for women's social, political, and economic equality as far from won", with Deborah Siegel commenting that "In the mid-1990s, as the postfeminists were busy pronouncing the personal no longer political, the newly self-identifying third wavers proclaimed the opposite."[21] Postfeminist culture and third-wave feminism do share certain commonalities – most notably the identification of women's sexual subjectivity as a crucial site of empowerment – yet postfeminism weds

DOI: 10.1057/9781137326546

notions of emancipation to consumer culture, with women's liberation "premised upon and enabled by the consumption of products and services, frequently associated with femininity/sexuality".[22]

In spite of these discernable differences, both postfeminism as a cultural condition and third-wave feminism as a political movement have allowed the expression and discussion of female sexuality to move beyond exclusively academic contexts and into mainstream popular culture and avant-garde subcultural production respectively. Yet, commenting on the difficulty of exploring and validating female sexuality in the context of social movements and organised political frameworks, Natasha Walter states that "the language of sexuality is individual, where as a political movement speaks a mass language; it is extraordinary, where as a political movement must be commonplace; it is private rather than public."[23] The following chapters of this book are thus committed to analysing the ways in which contemporary women express and live their individual, diverse and private sexual identities amidst conflicting narratives of female sexuality. This study is premised on the belief that contemporary erotic memoirs may have a special role to play in the process of reconfiguring female sexuality as active and agentic, offering an antidote to cultural elisions of female desire where the "vocabulary of sex is much more concerned with describing what happens to a man's body during sexual arousal than a woman's".[24] It is also premised on the conviction that, while offering private conceptualisations of female sexual subjectivity, women's memoirs are inherently political in their colonisation of the male dominated space within mass culture where mainstream narratives of human sexuality reside.

Naomi Wolf has commented that when narratives of sexuality are "attached to the lives of grown women, however tangentially, the associations undermine their authority",[25] thus demonstrating the political function that the publication of women's non-fictional sexual storytelling may play in recalibrating the taboo of women's sexual activity. While acknowledging that women's reclamation of the first-person sexual is filled with the potential for personal disaster, Wolf argues that a greater focus on narratives of sexual awakening is long overdue for "one can scarcely escape the male counterpart".[26] The publication of female sexual narratives is political, and not solely in terms of achieving representational parity in public narratives of sexual expression. Merri Lisa Johnson has noted the wider political importance of first-person narratives, commenting that "individual women's stories, narrow in scope and deep in

DOI: 10.1057/9781137326546

reflection, aid in advancing the complexity of feminist social theory",[27] while Jennifer Baumgardner and Amy Richards declare that "women's personal stories have been the evidence of where the movement needs to go politically".[28] First-person narratives have long been central to feminist consciousness-raising, and women's erotic memoirs in the 21st century are especially useful in terms of mapping the current status and interpretations of feminism within popular culture.

In this book, I seek to explore the conflict that arises when the female-authored memoir – a genre that holds enormous feminist potential – is coopted by postfeminist culture. The need to examine this point of friction – between feminist politics and postfeminist disavowal – is especially clear if we note that this contradiction often occurs within highly popular texts, suggesting that female consumers find, within this political impasse, acute resonance to their personal lived experiences. One only needs to look towards E.L. James' bestselling phenomenon *Fifty Shades of Grey* (2011) to realise the ubiquity of the postfeminist dilemma within the contemporary historical moment. Indeed, James' novel registers the strength and vitality of women in the aftermath of feminism, and yet simultaneously portrays them as coveting more traditional and reactionary gender regimes. The novel's protagonist, Anastasia Steele, is ostensibly independent and feisty, while her best friend Kate symbolises the emergence of the modern neo-liberal woman as a figure who has attended "the best private schools in Washington" and has "grown up confident and sure of her place in the world",[29] a woman whose "beauty and commanding manner disarm" the men whom she meets.[30] Anastasia is likewise described by Kate as "a total babe", and at various points in the novel her independence is highlighted: "You, fascinated by a man? That's a first."[31] Like all postfeminist heroines, Anastasia is strong and obstinate, and yet like all postfeminist heroines she is unable to resist the sexual appeal of a domineering male partner and is swept away in the ideologies of romantic love. Her demonstrations of independence prove to be little more than a facade, for even though many suspect she is "missing the need-a-boyfriend gene" she in actuality "longs for the fabled trembling knees, heart-in-my-mouth, butterflies-in-my-belly moments".[32] Christian Grey further disempowers Anastasia, for in his presence she becomes "gushing and breathy – like a child, not a grown woman who can vote and drink legally",[33] and he himself proves to be conventionally gendered despite gesturing towards the ownership of a metrosexual, postfeminist identity. Even though the author invests great

DOI: 10.1057/9781137326546

attention to describing his "beautifully manicured hands"[34] and tailored apparel, he remains conventionally masculine, "autocratic and cold",[35] a man who "[does not] do romance".[36] James reifies the reactionary erotic scripts of the romance genre, of dominant male and passive female subject positions, for Grey is, after all, a "mega-industrialist tycoon"[37] while Steele is an undergraduate student. This economic and political imbalance is paralleled in their sexual histories: Grey is vastly sexually experienced while Steele is a virgin. The latter reminds the reader of another virginal romantic heroine of postfeminist popular culture – Isabella Swan in Stephenie Meyer's *Twilight* series. Like Bella, Anastasia is characterised by contradiction, fluctuating between activity and passivity, and like Bella she is constructed as insecure, physically inept and socially awkward, someone who prefers to "sit inconspicuously at the back of the room".[38] Likewise, Grey parallels *Twilight*'s Edward Cullen, for while clearly not a vampire he performs similar, hyperbolic feats of heroic masculinity and demonstrates supreme physical prowess. Standing side by side, "awkwardly on [her] part, coolly self-possessed on [his]",[39] there is nothing neither feminist nor subversive about the power dynamic between Anastasia and Grey, despite the apparently empowering journey of erotic self-discovery subsequently undertaken by the protagonist.

Fifty Shades of Grey is a novel, not a memoir, and Anastasia is limited by her confinement within the conventions of the romance genre. Even though she motions towards agency, too much female agency exhibited within a romance narrative would be deemed an incongruous and a somewhat "unromantic" subversion of femininity, negating her appeal to the popular fiction consumer. In counterpoint, the memoirs discussed in this book free themselves of the gendered limitations of genre in the nebulous space they occupy as confessional accounts of "true" sexual encounters. As such, readers expect the authors to reject romantic conventions, and the clearest and most prevalent indication of this rejection is the persona of the "phallic girl" or "ladette" that dominates the majority of the texts under discussion. While this rejection of romance may allow the perceptive reader to position these memoirs as feminist statements, it is important to recognise, as Imelda Whelehan astutely observes, that the phallic girl "could only have emerged in an atmosphere hostile to feminism",[40] and her presence in any popular text is especially problematic when the female reader is encouraged to identify with her as a manifestation of "girl power". Whelehan situates the ladette

DOI: 10.1057/9781137326546

as a type of phallic girl who "adopts traditionally 'male' behaviour in an attempt to subvert or deflect male lechery".[41] Her dominance within the contemporary memoir is especially problematic if we accept Whelehan's conclusion that – defining the ladette as "part exposé of men's worst machismo, part attempt at appropriation of behaviours traditionally prescribed to women" – there is "nothing particularly liberating about such a persona".[42] Whelehan proceeds to assert that while the ladette may represent a "reversal of gender roles in their depiction of men as the objects of desire", such figures ultimately prove that in order to subvert stereotypes of masculinity and femininity one has to do much more than simply reverse the equation.[43] Likewise, this book argues that while the feminist potential of women's erotic memoirs appears to rest on the formulation of new, sexually empowered feminine subjectivities, this construction is undermined by the prevalence of the figure of the phallic girl.

Considering the ubiquity of not only the phallic girl persona, but also the popular diary form in which her narrative voice is articulated, the memoirs discussed in this book could be categorised as pertaining to the term "clit lit" – an expression occasionally employed in popular journalism both interchangeably and erroneously with the term "chick lit". If this inordinately distasteful term need ever be deployed, then it should be done so more accurately, perhaps as a way of identifying highly sexual narratives that replicate the formal aesthetics of chick lit. Similar to the protagonists of chick lit – defined by Caroline Smith as "young, single, white, heterosexual, British and American women in their late twenties and early thirties, living in metropolitan areas" – all of the memoirs discussed in this book are written by women who reside in London and New York, or – in the case of texts set in continental Europe – Milan and Paris. The narrators live within close proximity to the fashionable milieus of their respective cities, and are not only Caucasian but also of Asian ethnicity, supporting Smith's claim that the demographic for chick lit has expanded due to its commercial viability and now "chronicles the lives of women of varying ages, races, and nationalities".[44] The sexual content of contemporary erotic memoirs also permits the positioning of these texts alongside the "subordinated spaces"[45] of chick lit – the popular and the female – in accordance with the widespread conviction that erotic fiction is not "serious" literature.

According to Suzanne Ferris and Mallory Young, "chick lit features single women in their twenties and thirties navigating their generation's challenges of balancing demanding careers with personal relationships".[46] Whether employed as a call girl struggling to balance sex work and academic study (Belle de Jour's *The Intimate Adventures of a London Call Girl* [2005]; Miss S' *Confessions of a Working Girl* [2007]) or marriage (Tracy Quan's *Diary of a Married Call Girl* [2005]), the contemporary erotic memoir similarly aims to centralise authenticity and female address, and in doing so reflects the "lives of everyday working young women" searching for self-definition and stability amidst the conflicting narratives of heterosexual romance and feminist emancipation. Bearing in mind Imelda Whelehan's observation regarding the emergence of "mumlit" – "effectively the natural sequel to chick lit where the singleton grows up, settles down, and has her babies"[47] – it is perhaps not surprising that chick lit would evolve into "clit lit" in Western cultures that have become increasingly sexualised (Levy 2005, McRobbie 2009). Rosalind Gill has commented that even though "chick lit" characters are employed and committed to the idea of a career, most hold underpaid positions, "typical of the actual situation in which most working women are concentrated in low-paid jobs in the service sector".[48] In a similar manner, contemporary erotic memoirs appeal to the "normal" woman as they feature everyday women not only employed in underpaid but socially legitimate occupations, but women who are actively engaged in fully capitulating to popular culture's prevailing message that the most successful way for women to become financially empowered – and therefore liberated – is through the cultivation of an active and hedonistic sexuality.

This book focuses on the figure of the sexually active, and ostensibly "empowered" female protagonist in a number of mass-market and literary memoirs. The extent to which these memoirs are accurate, truthful and valid accounts of sexual histories is, of course, impossible to ascertain. I contend that the majority are highly fictionalised accounts of sexual desire and sexual practice, however it is important to note that all of the following texts under discussion are marketed as non-fiction memoirs: Jenny Angell's *Callgirl* (2007), Toni Bentley's *The Surrender: An Erotic Memoir* (2006), Belle de Jour's *The Intimate Adventures of a London Call Girl* (2005), Almudena Grandes' *The Ages of Lulu* (1993), Krissy Kneen's *Affection: An Erotic Memoir* (2010), Abby Lee's *Girl with a One Track Mind: Confessions of the Seductress Next Door* (2006), Sienna Lewis' *Intimate Adventures of an Office Girl* (2009), Melissa P's *One Hundred Strokes of the Brush Before Bed* (2004), Catherine Millet's *The Sexual*

DOI: 10.1057/9781137326546

Life of Catherine M. (2002), Miss S' *Confessions of a Working Girl* (2007),
Dawn Porter's *Diaries of an Internet Lover* (2006), Suzanne Portnoy's
The Butcher, the Baker, the Candlestick Maker (2006)/*The Not So Invisible
Woman* (2008), Tracy Quan's *Diary of a Manhattan Call Girl* (2001)/*Diary
of a Married Call Girl* (2005), and Catherine Townsend's *Sleeping Around:
Secrets of a Sexual Adventuress* (2007)/*Breaking the Rules: Confessions of a
Bad Girl* (2008).

The first chapter of this book is concerned with analysing the manner in which women's memoirs validate sexual assertion as the primary
means of empowerment and agency. Mindful of Janet Holland's observation that feminine sexualities in Western cultures are constructed in
subordination to dominant masculine sexualities (Holland 1996), this
chapter explores how postfeminist culture encourages women to subvert
this pattern by forcefully expressing their sexual expectations and desires.
While recognising that contemporary women do powerfully voice
concerns regarding their own sexual desires, this chapter suggests that
postfeminist sensibilities of choice and empowerment are complicit in
masking a social reality in which little has changed in terms of real-world
sexual practices and power relations. Simply put, that while contemporary women may express what they desire sexually and promote parity
between the sexes, this vision of sexual equality and liberation seldom
transpires in practice, and descriptions of sexual encounters position
women's sexual pleasure as secondary to men's. The chapter argues that
this discord – between the conceptual representation of sexual politics
and the material representation of sexual practices – can be understood
as an outcome of the competing discourses of popular feminism and the
mainstreaming of the sex industry.

The second chapter further focuses on the relationship between
postfeminist culture and the mainstreaming of the sex industry, paying
particular attention to new constructions of sexual intimacy in the 21st
century. It seeks to determine if women's erotic memoirs locate sexual
intimacy as predicated on traditional scripts of love and romance, or if
postfeminist "raunch culture" has entirely coopted feminist resistance
to traditional relationships by positioning sexual promiscuity as a valid
mode of empowerment. The chapter argues that the dominance of
traditional romantic and monogamous sexual relationships in women's
lives has been destabilised by the emergence of "hookup" sex, a term and
behaviour which Gail Dines positions as an outcome of the mainstreaming of the sex industry. It pursues this line of enquiry by demonstrating

DOI: 10.1057/9781137326546

how the memoirs position commercial and non-commercial sexual encounters in close proximity, as sites where emotional and physical intimacies are similarly produced and consumed. The chapter concludes by suggesting that contemporary erotic memoirs espouse a number of contradictory messages, with some identifying sexual pleasure as form of neo-liberal politics, and others remaining bound in romantic ideologies that construct sex and love as interdependent. In addition, it suggests that the growth of the Internet has had a dramatic effect on women's understanding of intimacy and sexual behaviour.

The third chapter of this book attempts to position the memoirs in the nebulous space between "pornography" and "erotica". Erotica is a genre that is textual rather than visual, primarily female authored rather than male produced, and created with an elite audience in mind. Pornography, by contrast, is commonly associated with visual culture and produced by men for the mass consumption of a predominantly male audience. The chapter argues that while the female-authored erotic memoir is a genre inherently concordant with erotica, postfeminist culture and the mainstreaming of pornography have coopted and colonised the form. The chapter suggests that women's erotic memoirs inhabit a space that is both progressive and regressive – a challenge to and an affirmation of the aesthetics of pornography – the former by forcefully expressing a postfeminist female agency in the (visual) consumption of male and female bodies, and the latter by adhering to the conventions of male-produced pornography. It argues that while the memoirs certainly demonstrate women's pleasure in "consuming" and "performing" pornography, an adherence to the sexual and narrative paradigms of pornography complicates attempts to present both the active female body and female written testimony as markers of sexual agency.

The final chapter focuses on the manner in which erotic memoirs understand sexual desire as constitutionally subversive, and therefore inherently difficult to place in harmonious concordance with any political or ideological framework. Recognising that sexual experiences are unavoidably political as powerful agents for subverting social norms and institutional values, this chapter argues that sexual desire and behaviour is often resistant to "traditional" or "politically correct" feminist politics. As such, it demonstrates how many of the memoirs position violence – both received and enacted – as a necessary and even desired component of sexual practice, locating the memoirs' attitudes to sexual violence in both postfeminist culture and third-wave feminist ideology. Finally, it

DOI: 10.1057/9781137326546

suggests that women's erotic memoirs engage in a process of normalising and destigmatising not only ostensibly transgressive female behaviour, such as sexual promiscuity, but even more extreme forms of taboo sexuality such as sadomasochism, prostitution and paedophilia.

Notes

1 Joseph Bristow, *Sexuality* (London and New York: Routledge, 1997), 1.

2 Jeffrey Weeks, *Sexuality* (London and New York: Routledge, 2003), 105.

3 Ibid.

4 Ibid.

5 Ibid., 106.

6 Gayle Rubin, "Thinking Sex: Notes for a Radical Theory of the Politics of Sexuality" in *Pleasure and Danger: Exploring Female Sexuality*, ed. Carol Vance (London: Pandora Press, 1989), 278.

7 Jeffrey Weeks, *Invented Moralities: Sexual Values in an Age of Uncertainty* (New York: Columbia University Press, 1995), 48.

8 Rosalind Coward, "Sex after Aids" in *Feminism and Sexuality: A Reader*, eds Stevi Jackson and Sue Scott (Edinburgh: Edinburgh University Press, 1996), 246.

9 Chris Beasley, *Gender and Sexuality: Critical Theories, Critical Thinkers* (London: Sage, 2005), 117.

10 Lynne Segal, *Is the Future Female?: Troubled Thoughts on Contemporary Feminism* (London: Virago, 1987), 75.

11 Carol Vance, "Pleasure and Danger: Towards a Politics of Sexuality" in *Pleasure and Danger: Exploring Female Sexuality*, ed. Carol Vance (London: Pandora Press, 1989), 4.

12 Segal, *Is the Future Female?* 72.

13 Ibid., 78.

14 Sarah Projansky, *Watching Rape: Film and Television in Postfeminist Culture* (New York: New York University Press, 2001), 89.

15 Ibid., 68.

16 Stephanie Genz and Benjamin Brabon, *Postfeminism: Cultural Texts and Theories* (Edinburgh: Edinburgh University Press, 2009), 1.

17 Ibid., 6.

18 Angela McRobbie, *The Aftermath of Feminism: Gender, Culture and Social Change* (London: Sage, 2009), 11.

19 Genz and Brabon, *Postfeminism*, 81.

20 Ibid., 70.

21 Deborah Siegel, *Sisterhood, Interrupted: From Radical Women to Grrrls Gone Wild* (Basingstoke: Palgrave Macmillan, 2007), 132.

DOI: 10.1057/9781137326546

22   Genz and Brabon, *Postfeminism*, 79.
23   Natasha Walter, *The New Feminism* (London: Virago, 1999), 121–122.
24   Diane Richardson, "Constructing Lesbian Identities" in *Feminism and Sexuality: A Reader*, eds Stevi Jackson and Sue Scott (Edinburgh: Edinburgh University Press, 1996), 279.
25   Naomi Wolf, *Promiscuities: A Secret History of Female Desire* (London: Vintage, 1998), 5.
26   Ibid., 6.
27   Merri Lisa Johnson, "Jane Hocus, Jane Focus" in *Jane Sexes It Up: True Confessions of Feminist Desire*, ed. Merri Lisa Johnson (New York: Four Walls Eight Windows, 2002), 5.
28   Jennifer Baumgardner and Amy Richards, *Manifesta: Young Women, Feminism and the Future* (New York: Farrar, Straus and Giroux, 2010 [2000]), 20.
29   E.L. James, *Fifty Shades of Grey* (New York: Vintage, 2012), 37.
30   Ibid., 36.
31   Ibid., 21.
32   Ibid., 24.
33   Ibid., 35.
34   Ibid., 26.
35   Ibid., 17.
36   Ibid., 72.
37   Ibid., 3.
38   Ibid., 6.
39   Ibid., 16.
40   Imelda Whelehan, *Overloaded: Popular Culture and the Future of Feminism* (London: The Women's Press, 2000), 15.
41   Ibid., 50.
42   Ibid.
43   Ibid., 51.
44   Caroline Smith, *Cosmopolitan Culture and Consumerism in Chick Lit* (London and New York: Routledge, 2008), 2.
45   Ibid., 4.
46   Mallory Young and Suzanne Ferriss, *Chick Lit: The New Woman's Fiction* (London and New York: Routledge, 2005), 3.
47   Imelda Whelehan, *The Feminist Bestseller* (Basingstoke: Palgrave Macmillan, 2005), 194.
48   Rosalind Gill, *Gender and the Media* (Cambridge: Polity Press, 2006), 237.

DOI: 10.1057/9781137326546

1

Agency

Abstract: *The first chapter analyses the manner in which women's erotic memoirs validate sexual assertion as a form of empowerment and agency. While femininity and feminine sexualities in Western cultures have generally been positioned by a number of contemporary feminists as disempowering and constructed in subordination to dominant masculine sexualities, this chapter explores how postfeminist culture extolls women who subvert this pattern by forcefully expressing their sexual expectations and desires. While recognising that contemporary women do assert their sexual desires, this chapter suggests that postfeminist sensibilities of choice and empowerment are complicit in masking a social reality in which little has changed in terms of real-world sexual practices.*

Gwynne, Joel. *Erotic Memoirs and Postfeminism: The Politics of Pleasure*. Basingstoke: Palgrave Macmillan, 2013. DOI: 10.1057/9781137326546.

Since the late 1960s, feminists have exposed the complexity and ubiquity of power within heterosexual relations. Over the course of the past 40 years, it has been clearly and resolutely argued that desire as socially constituted, whether lesbian or heterosexual, is inevitably gendered, and that heterosexual desire is premised on gender difference; on the sexual "otherness" of the desired object. This difference is not an anatomical one but a social one, a hierarchy of gender, since it is gender hierarchy which renders anatomical differences socially and erotically significant.[1] In the 21st century, we have witnessed a seismic shift in the manner in which desire – specifically female desire – is constructed and represented in visual and written forms. Female desire is now invariably read in the context of female empowerment, and often through the critical vernacular of postfeminism; a much contested and nebulous term in itself. Sarah Gamble's definition of postfeminism as "women dressing like bimbos, yet claiming male privileges and attitudes"[2] demonstrates the strength of some feminists' scepticism, which often derives from challenging any conceptualisation of the term as representing a movement that strives for equality between the sexes.

Gamble astutely observes that "postfeminism" is often barricaded in inverted commas, suggesting that critics are not only wary of positioning the term as representing definite and resolute feminist values, but are even unsure as to whether the term represents a "con trick engineered by the media or a valid movement".[3] The difficulty in locating postfeminism as a valid movement is largely due to two determining factors. First, there is an absence of unified feminist values and sensibilities in the multitude of mediums and contexts in which postfeminist thought is expressed. This is largely because it is "skewed in favour of liberal humanism" and embraces a "flexible ideology which can be adapted to suit individual needs and desires".[4] Second, and perhaps most important of all, many feminists who align themselves to more traditional forms of feminism reject postfeminism by identifying it as a betrayal of a history of feminist struggle, a "rejection of all it has gained".[5] Due to the visible success of past feminist movements, contemporary British culture presents a plethora of social contexts that have proven fertile ground for the growth of postfeminist forms of empowerment. In *Living Dolls: The Return of Sexism* (2010), Natasha Walter charts a highly sexualised culture in which the constant reinforcement of one type of role model is "shrinking and warping" the choices on offer to young women. Indeed, the author comments that "sexualised images of young women are threatening to squeeze

DOI: 10.1057/9781137326546

out other kinds of images of women throughout popular culture",[6] and attributes this shift to the fact that prostitution and the values of the sex industry have "moved from the margins to the mainstream".[7] This can be seen not only through the publication of numerous bestselling accounts of prostitution, such as Belle de Jour's *The Intimate Adventures of a London Call Girl* (2005), but through the publication of books marketed as non-fictional erotic memoirs of educated career women who are not prostitutes. More often than not, these accounts are identified as an indication of the strength of postfeminist culture; its celebration of female sexual empowerment and "refusal of any definition of women as victims who are unable to control their own lives".[8] Indeed, just as postfeminism is inclined to be "unwilling to condemn pornography",[9] recent erotic memoirs demonstrate a challenge to sexual absolutism or those who may pass judgement on any facet of women's sexual decision-making. In this chapter, I will explore the following question: Do these memoirs celebrate women's autonomous negotiation of sexual decision-making or, conversely, do they reflect a saturation of, and submission to, male-dominated sexual values ascribed by the popularisation and mainstreaming of the sex industry? I will aim to answer this question by focusing on two interlinked thematic strands: the conceptual representation of sexual politics, and the material representation of sexual practices.

Sexual politics

In *The New Feminism* (1999), Walter condemns the occasional hysteria of second-wave feminist thought, commenting that in the 1970s "all treatments of sexuality in culture were forced to reveal the imprint of sexism: fairy tales, fiction high and low, erotica, cinema, photography, sculpture", concluding that a minority of feminists perceived "any hint of sexuality in culture" as "proof of sexism".[10] Now, in the 21st century, the representation of dominant female sexuality, across all mediums of visual and textual expression, predominantly avoids the usual cultural trap of promiscuity; the image of the uncontrolled nymphomaniac. Just as contemporary popular culture is more receptive to female sexual expression, feminist critical discourse has become more tolerant to the liberating possibilities of heterosexual relations, with feminists such as Walter asserting that any insistence on perceiving heterosexual culture

DOI: 10.1057/9781137326546

as a threat to female agency entails losing "the great power that women have often felt in that world".[11] Similar to Gamble's assertion of post-feminism as an ethos inseparable from liberal humanism, Walter argues that unless the potential advantages of heterosexual relations are fully realised, feminists "run the risk of placing women as victims even when they are not".[12]

It is this climate of active female sexual expression and a more inclusive feminist discourse that has seen recent erotic non-fiction memoirs thrive. Suzanne Portnoy's bestseller *The Butcher, the Baker, the Candlestick Maker* (2006) successfully captures the *zeitgeist* of postfeminist sexual assertion. Portnoy is "not in the market for a boyfriend" but rather "in the market for getting what [she] want[s]".[13] Her circle of friends and female support-network espouse a personal philosophy that "men shouldn't get a name",[14] and therefore an identity, until they have had sex with Portnoy three times, reducing them first and foremost to sexual objects. On the subject of casual sex, Portnoy makes it clear that "freedom means sex",[15] and sexual activity is positioned as a counterpoint to the traditional role of a mother that she previously occupied: "One thing is clear, however: not getting fucked at all is not an option. I love sex. My kids-free Friday nights come along just twice a month, and I have to take advantage of them."[16] The importance of sex extends beyond pleasure, and is employed as a direct tool of empowerment, evident in her recollection of a sexual experience at university: "I fucked him because he looked arrogant and I thought it would be satisfying to demolish his ego."[17] There is no clarification regarding how, exactly, this aim is achieved through intercourse, but the intent is clear: for Portnoy, sex, freedom and power are interdependent.

The explicit link made by Portnoy between an ethos of postfeminist sexual liberation and freedom is precipitated by a frustration towards a reactionary culture that still upholds the values of sexual essentialism: a belief in the deep, unchanging character of innate sexuality. This frustration and a move towards egalitarianism between the sexes based on mutual understanding are sentiments that bind many recent erotic memoirs. In Abby Lee's *Girl with a One Track Mind: Confessions of the Seductress Next Door* (2006), the author (Zoe Margolis) comments that it is "still largely unacceptable for men to admit to [an] emotional need in case they are labeled 'weak' or 'feminine', and if a woman is open about her sexual desires she's instantly a 'slut' ", isolating this disparity in

DOI: 10.1057/9781137326546

gender stereotypes as a "source of conflict between the sexes".[18] She proceeds to promote the tenets of egalitarianism: "In my experience men want and need love and companionship just as much as their female counterparts and women seek sexual pleasure and gratification just as much as men do."[19] While hardly a ground-breaking observation, the text nevertheless functions to present accessible feminist politics to the popular reader.

Catherine Townsend's *Sleeping Around: Secrets of a Sexual Adventuress* (2007) demonstrates a similar hostility to gendered misconceptions and double standards, namely that "a woman who has loads of sexual partners is still seen as a slapper, while guys who hook up constantly are considered studs",[20] and asserts: "I don't think it's unreasonable to expect a little mutual pleasure and respect, even from a casual fling."[21] This movement towards greater parity in sexual relations is even evident in the memoir's appropriation of the historically male terrain of anatomical objectification. In *Getting Off: Pornography and the End of Masculinity* (2007), Robert Jensen states that: "One of the common discussions men have – and one that perplexed me even before I had any critical consciousness around these issues – is about what kind of bodies and body parts they like and what specific sex acts they enjoy."[22] The consensus that body parts and sexual acts can be isolated attests to a culture in which sex is often divorced from emotional intimacy, and Townsend affirms a similar viewpoint after an encounter with a man with a small penis: "A massive member may not be essential for me, but a tiny one is, alas, a deal-breaker. Since men have no qualms about stating their preferences for purely aesthetic characteristics such as big breasts or a slim figure, I don't think that women should feel guilty about admitting to their own needs."[23] The sexual encounter is void of emotional intimacy and, just as in male discourses of sexuality, anatomical preference takes precedence.

The female voice is no longer silent, and in tracing the (re)configurations of the women's movement from its genesis to the present day, Walter's *The New Feminism* (1999) celebrated the current political climate, emphasising how the vocalisation of female sexual desire has become the *sine qua non* of contemporary society.[24] Yet, in her later book *Living Dolls: The Return of Sexism* (2010), Walter argues that women's authentic expression of sexual desire has become co-opted by a culture of hypersexuality. In terms of authorship and the public female voice, Abby Lee's memoir demonstrates the difficulty that women may still experience

DOI: 10.1057/9781137326546

when attempting to discuss sexuality. In fact, Lee declares that her desire to write a memoir is motivated by the limitations placed on women's sexual dialogue, even in the company of close female friends:

> My own friends appear quite happy to sit in a pub, swapping *Sex and the City* anecdotes and joking about rabbit vibrators. But, the thing is, if I get into more detail and mention something like, say, wanting to try out a cock ring on a guy while fingering his arse, they all suddenly become rather quiet or jump up and volunteer to buy the next round.[25]

Female sexual expression is socially restricted, and is usually confined within a commercialised perception of sexual liberation that circumnavigates frank discussions of sexual preference. This is partly a consequence of the fact that social relations and female kinship remain imbricated with cultural discourses of sexuality that are qualified by the scripts of romantic love[26] and long-term commitment: "I wish I could just be myself and talk openly with them, but how can I be truthful and tell them I want to try out group sex when they only seem to care about finding that one special man to have sex with?"[27] Thus, for Lee, female authorship, and retreating into the private sphere by writing an anonymous memoir, becomes the only permissible and authentic mode of expressing desire: "I reckoned that writing everything down would be the only way I could be truly open about sex; I could talk about my sexuality and desires as a woman and not have to worry or care what people might think, and whether they'd judge me or not. It would be liberating."[28]

The emphasis on redirecting female expression to the realm of sexual intimacy, rather than emotional intimacy, accords with contemporary feminist positions on heterosexual romance, which often implicate love between men and women as detrimental since it encourages women to "give up their won power and fall into the hands of the enemy".[29] Indeed, it is the repudiation of romantic love that, above all other aspects, connects the memoirs of Lee, Townsend and Portnoy, and where concordance in their sexual politics is achieved. Portnoy renders the link between romantic love and a loss of self. Prior to marriage she was a "pushy New York Jewish broad turned London punkette",[30] a woman who was perceived as "least likely to have children, because [she] never expressed much interest in kids or seemed particularly maternal".[31] After marriage, she sublimates her unconventionality in her role as a "generic mother and ignored wife",[32] and eventually becomes the "frumpy, overweight, undersexed mother [she'd] seen all [her] life in the grocery stores".[33] After

DOI: 10.1057/9781137326546

divorcing her husband, she enters casual relationships absolved of the difficult terrain of emotional intimacy and commitment: "I didn't have all the usual girlfriend problems, all the things chicks worry about: when I'd see him next, whether he'd phone me, how much he liked me."[34]

Similar to Townsend's forthright anatomical focalisation, Portnoy's rejection of romantic ideology manifests itself as a rejection of emotional intimacy. Yet, her position implies a resigned acceptance of this stance, and functions as a counterpoint to Townsend's celebratory tone: "When girls are younger, we all think every man who fucks us is a potential husband. It took me a long time to figure out that most of them just want to get laid – and nothing more. Now I feel the same way they do."[35] The social construction of heterosexual romance is directly challenged further by Townsend, who spends Valentine's Day with her female friend drinking Love Bird Specials while "discussing how women's emotional expectations are raised to unrealistic levels by a diet of romance novels".[36] She comments on how her rejection of this construction began at a young age when playing with a Barbie doll as a child: "My Barbie is rich and famous and has two Kens."[37] Ultimately, it is the rejection of heterosexual romantic love that can be identified as the catalyst of postfeminist sexual decision-making, with Townsend concluding that sometimes all a woman needs is a "semi-literate fuck machine",[38] and Lee proclaiming: "Why search for a knight in shining armour when you can have a great ride with just a few vodka-based cocktails and a cheap sex toy to hand?"[39] Yet, despite this allegiance to postfeminist rhetoric, it is highly significant that by the end of the memoirs of Lee, Townsend and Portnoy, all women ultimately seek *both* emotional and sexual intimacy with a long-term partner. This narrative turn positions the texts close to the ideals of romantic love that the authors ostensibly renounce, and that women have historically been encouraged to aspire to, implicating promiscuity as an in-road, rather than a final destination, in the journey to self-fulfilment.

Sexual practices

The evaluation of the sexual politics of three contemporary erotic memoirs has revealed postfeminism's mark in a number of ways. We have witnessed women's forthright desire for sex without emotional intimacy, asserted through written and verbal expression. We have witnessed a

DOI: 10.1057/9781137326546

refusal to be drawn into the sacrifices that women often make for men in the name of romantic love. We have witnessed the reduction of men to sexual objects, and a centralisation of male anatomical attributes. Yet, in "Pressured Pleasure: Young Women and the Negotiation of Sexual Boundaries", Holland *et al.* observe that "Empowerment at the intellectual level does not mean that young women can achieve empowerment in subsequent sexual encounters."[40] They proceed to highlight the feminist sensibilities required to ensure that empowerment can occur in real-world encounters, stating that women can only assert sexual needs in terms of their own bodily pleasure if they "stand up to, if not go against" the boundaries of femininity in sexual relationships, since "a positive femininity is a challenge to dominant masculinities".[41] There is, of course, no doubt that all three memoirs convey the distinct impression of 21st century women in control of their sexual expression. Yet, pursuing the line of enquiry asserted by Holland *et al.*, we have not witnessed how these attitudes are played out in terms of sexual practices. Simply put, to what extent do the authors of these memoirs put into practice the confidence, dominance and self-assertion they display in their sexual politics? Are the politics of the bedroom as egalitarian as their postfeminist sensibilities seem to imply?

According to Holland *et al.*, effective empowerment in sexual negotiations manifests itself in a number of ways, through "not engaging in sexual activity; not engaging in sexual activity without informed consent; getting men to consent for safer practices; negotiating sexual practices which are pleasurable to women as well as to men".[42] Employing these criteria as a guideline it is clear that the memoirs, albeit only to a certain extent, affirm certain forms of female empowerment. Portnoy demonstrates informed consent: "How far I let them go depends on how attractive I find them. Most times I remove their hand from my leg and that's where it ends."[43] Townsend demonstrates active control over safe-sex practices, even when men absolve themselves of this responsibility, commenting that "as a student at New York University, [she] carried condoms in a chic and discreet vintage Gucci purse" and lamenting that "British men tend never to mention safe sex or use condoms, at least not without [her] insistence".[44] In addition, both Portnoy and Townsend demand sexual practices that are pleasurable to women, even though these demands are met with primarily disappointing results. After Portnoy suggests oral sex to her partner, he "looked horrified [...] either he'd never met a woman who'd communicated what she wanted in bed,

DOI: 10.1057/9781137326546

or he was appalled at the idea of cunnilingus".[45] Townsend experiences similar difficulties when she masturbates in bed after failing to achieve orgasm, even with the assistance of Viagra: "Baby, I'm not quite finished yet," I said. "I hope you don't mind if I touch myself"'.[46] Her partner recoils, exclaiming "Nice girls don't do those things. My attitude with orgasms is if they happen, they happen. Maybe it's just not meant to be."[47] These examples reveal that even though empowerment is not always achieved, the authors do at least attempt to negotiate sexual boundaries, documenting contemporary women's shifting expectations.

Portnoy, Townsend and Lee sustain this attitude throughout their memoirs. Lee's memoir champions equity in sexual negotiations in a manner that accords with her postfeminist sensibilities. Her perception of intercourse is reciprocal and based on mutual understanding, and she reflects on a period in her youth when she was unable to achieve an orgasm: "Since I didn't even know how to bring myself off at that point, there was no point expecting him to be able to get me there."[48] Similarly, Portnoy reflects on a disappointing encounter that failed to result in mutual satisfaction: "If I were a hooker, it would have been fine that he'd made no effort to satisfy me."[49] Prior to this, during her marriage, she also failed to achieve sexual parity: "The sex was fine during our first six months together but, as on the first night we slept together, I was always the one making the first move, and after a while being the initiator ceased to be fun."[50] All of these examples demonstrate that mutual sexual satisfaction and the mutual initiation of intercourse are expected as fundamental components of modern intimate relationships. This is occasionally achieved, and in relaying her sexual encounters Portnoy states, "I looked at his hard cock and then knelt down and put it in my mouth. 'Plenty of time for that later', he said. 'You know how quickly I come. Sit on my face instead.'"[51] Here, her desire to satisfy her lover is reciprocated. On occasions where men do not accommodate her desire, Portnoy is forthright: "I figured I'd grind on his face and have my own orgasm within five minutes."[52] Even so, it can be argued that these occasions, where empowerment and mutual satisfaction are achieved, form the exception rather than the rule.

Certainly, for there are many occasions in the memoirs where the authors confuse female empowerment with male model empowerment. Holland *et al.* argue that "In the context of sexual encounters, empowering women need not mean women exerting power over men, or behaving like men. We have conceptualized this as a 'male model empowerment' and have categorized it as a form of disempowerment for women."[53] Similar to Townsend's anatomical itemisation of the male form, Portnoy extolls sexual practices that are not always pleasurable to men, and therefore parallels the dissatisfaction that women have often experienced in sexual relations where female satisfaction is not valued and accommodated: "Like an obedient puppy, he showed up, on the dot. I sat on his cock until I came, then pulled him out and jerked him off. After he came, I said, 'OK, you have to go now. I'm really busy'."[54] Lee observes a paid-sex encounter between a female dominatrix and a male client: "She then instructed him to climax on cue, and so he grabbed his cock and wanked himself off in front of us, finally climaxing as she commanded. He spunked a wad all over her latex-clad hand, which she then shoved into his mouth."[55] While Lee presents this act as empowering, for the experience makes her "intrigued about experimenting with a little light S&M",[56] it is debatable if this eroticisation of power, especially forcing the swallowing of semen, is indeed empowering for women.

The eroticisation of power is, of course, divisive territory, yet Walter has warned that feminist discourse should now, in the 21st century, be wary of colonising women's sexual experiences. She argues that the language of sexuality is individual, whereas feminism "speaks a mass language", and that given the cultural acceptance of women's public discourse and the pluralism of contemporary sexual mores, feminists should not "reduce all the tangles that heterosexual women live through to the dead weight of patriarchy".[57] Historically, the tradition of erotic writing has often celebrated sex as danger and transgression, and contemporary feminists such as Patrick Califia[58] defend even sadomasochistic sexual relations: "People choose to endure pain or discomfort if the goal they are striving for makes it worthwhile [...] The fact that masochism is disapproved of when stressful physical activity and religious martydom are not is an interesting example of the way sex is made a special case in our society."[59] Like Califia, Townsend makes a similar point in her memoir, arguing that she is "always surprised when people referred to certain sexual practices as anti-feminist, because what's most erotic is not necessarily the most politically correct",[60] echoing Lynne Segal's observation that human sexuality is "generated by, and in the service of, a multitude of needs, not all of them nice".[61]

Pornography is one such sphere, and written testimonies of male-dominated sexual encounters where female sexual pleasure is marginal heavily implicate the mainstreaming of the sex industry. The production

DOI: 10.1057/9781137326546

and consumption of pornography has always been a contentious and debated issue in feminist discourse, however Walter argues that "the classic feminist critique of pornography had left something very important out: it assumed that women never take any pleasure in pornography."[62] Townsend affirms such a perspective, stating that: "I was surprised to hear that porn was still a bit of a taboo subject. Amy always quotes Naomi Wolf, who argued that porn ultimately turns men off real women. I find her argument a bit simplistic: I've never met one for whom a pixilated image wasn't secondary to the real thing."[63] Perhaps Townsend's statement is also a little too simplistic, and fails to take into account the manner in which pornographic acts are imitated, produced and simulated in real-world sexual encounters,[64] especially since this simulacrum of desire is performed by Townsend herself: "I wetted my lips and consumed him, all the way to the back of my throat like a porn star."[65]

It could be argued that no individual should possess the moral authority to comment on another individual's sexual practices or decision making. Yet, if critics are to fully understand whether postfeminism is indeed an individual, liberal humanist sensibility that signifies a rejection of second-wave feminist achievements, or a sensibility that validates and fortifies the politics of second-wave feminism, an examination of the sexual lives of women cannot be suspended. Nor can we ignore the fact that, primarily but by no means exclusively, the memoirs of Townsend, Lee and Portnoy attest to a classic submission to heterosexual male dominance, even when flamboyantly championing the rhetoric of postfeminism. They do so by celebrating the values of the sex industry that fortify sexual inequalities, such as the practice that heterosexual intercourse must be penetrative and male-dominated in order to be pleasurable. In one particular sexual encounter, Portnoy reflects: "I felt myself getting wet, enjoying the domination. After months of keeping up the act, having to be the strong one all the time, I wanted to relinquish control."[66] In a further, extended and graphic description, Portnoy revels in submitting entirely to pleasuring, and being pleasured by, the penis:

> I love the responsiveness of a cock; the way it slides in and out of my mouth; the way I can make it do what I want it to do. I think about how it must feel when my tongue circles around the head and when I take it deep into my mouth until I almost gag. I slide my tongue up and down the shaft and then back into my mouth again. In my mind, I'm so connected to the man's cock, I get wetter and wetter and almost come myself, just thinking about what he must be feeling. My head moves up and down, up and down. Then

DOI: 10.1057/9781137326546

> I massage the head of his cock again, swirling my tongue, watching and feeling him get harder and harder.[67]

Portnoy is aroused despite almost choking on the penis, and stimulated even to the point of almost reaching climax in the absence of direct contact with her vagina or clitoris. Her hyperbolic desire is entirely male centred, and is precipitated by "thinking about what he must be feeling". Like Portnoy, Townsend demonstrates complete submission to male-centred sexual practices: "I learned that being submissive ultimately gave me great power. And although I was too wrapped up in his fantasies to focus on my own climax – that would come later – I was learning an incredible amount, and couldn't get enough."[68] Contemporary feminists will surely respond strongly to such a passage, for the erotic still arouses acute moral anxiety; historically, it has been difficult for critics to avoid passing moral judgement when examining the power relations of heterosexual intercourse. Yet, it is certainly possible to argue that, morality politics aside, contemporary erotic memoirs bear witness to not only male-dominated sexual relations, but more crucially, instances where male domination is certainly *not* an enjoyable experience for women. At a different point in the memoir, Portnoy demonstrates a lack of control in the negotiation of sexual boundaries with her long-term partner: "One morning, I lay in bed next to him, thinking, if he fucks me up the ass one more time, I'm going to scream."[69] After her partner tutors her on how to arouse men, she demonstrates a further lack of autonomy in choosing her attire: " 'What women never understand,' he said, 'is that the biggest turn-on for men isn't skimpy panties but no knickers at all.' Ever since he'd told me that, I never wore knickers under dresses or skirts."[70]

Portnoy's deference to male sexual power is further displayed when her partner "mounts [her] from behind, doggy style, and slips his cock inside".[71] This position of physical submission, while not necessarily counterproductive to female pleasure, is in this instance male centred, a position "almost guaranteed to get a guy off" as it "facilitates deep penetration", "looks hot from the man's perspective", and "gives the guy total control".[72] Despite her physical submission and male-centred psychological orientation, Portnoy feels her partner losing his erection. In an effort to stay aroused, he begins verbally abusing her, saying "the usual stuff: 'You're such a slut', he growls. 'I bet you really like being fucked by guys. Lots of guys. Lots and lots of guys.' "[73] Portnoy has become, at this stage in her life and in the memoir, desensitised to this form of verbal sexual abuse, and responds with indifference: "In my head I'm preparing

DOI: 10.1057/9781137326546

the vegetable curry I've earmarked for dinner the next day."[74] Thus, the reader witnesses not only submission to physical and verbal abuse, but in Portnoy's resigned acceptance of such behaviour, the suggestion that women should expect this treatment in sexual encounters and find such experiences tedious rather than alarming. On a less extreme scale, Townsend recalls a lover who "put [her] through the paces of light sub-mission and domination – or at least his version, which included being tied up with magician's rope, blind folded, with his cock in [her] mouth".[75] The emphasis here on "his version" is critical, and demonstrates the lack of control she experiences in these encounters, all of which fail to make her climax or even aroused. Thus, even when there is no absolute reason why sexual encounters need to necessarily position women as passive, or privilege certain male dominant sexual acts above others, or even why the act of sexual intercourse has to be configured as penetra-tive, the majority of popular women's memoirs refuse to avoid the trap of perpetuating this traditional pattern. Most significantly, despite the absence of pleasure in the huge number of sexual encounters described in recent memoirs, male power remains constitutionally eroticised and wholly unchallenged.

The memoirs of Lee, Portnoy and Townsend testify to significant changes in female sexual expression, yet in order to determine just how "progressive" these texts are it is essential to turn our attention to their conclusions. Portnoy's text ends with the narrator beginning a relation-ship with a man who entirely controls their sexual encounters: "I felt a bit like a human blow-up sex doll, passively doing as I was told. I was Karume's porn-fantasy woman, always complying, never resisting. And it was great."[76] After realising that "he wasn't Mr Right",[77] a phrase that reveals the narrator's unconscious adherence to traditional romantic scripts, Portnoy is "back on the market"[78] at the close of the memoir, searching for more sexual adventures in the context of non-commitment. Portnoy's decision to turn to sexual promiscuity to compensate for the absence of emotional intimacy, rather than presenting promiscuity as a lifestyle choice and cognizant political alternative, can be contrasted with the final pages of Lee's narrative: "I have come to the conclusion that even the best sex in the world can be unfulfilling in the long term. I need something more now."[79] The ending of Townsend's text can be located as an integration of the positions of both Lee and Portnoy, with the narrator espousing sexual promiscuity as well as emotional attach-ment: "In the past few months I've found someone to give me emotional

DOI: 10.1057/9781137326546

support, multiple orgasms, a shoulder to cry on, and physical bliss. So what if they weren't all with the same guy?"[80] By rejecting what she terms "the cookie-cutter fairy tale happy ending"[81] through locating sexual and emotional fulfilment across multiple partners, Townsend's memoir ends in the most progressive manner, and certainly seems to be the most politically aware of all of the texts discussed in this chapter.

While it is easy to criticise Portnoy and Lee's adherence to male-dominated romantic and sexual scripts, it is perhaps also important to adopt a more forgiving stance, one that acknowledges contemporary culture's complex attitudes to women in sexual and romantic relationships. Whether seeking, on the one hand, romantic and emotional fulfilment or, on the other, an exclusively sexual exchange, women all too easily fall prey to criticism for either conforming to patriarchal romantic narratives that entrap women or, alternatively, for conforming to the male fantasy of sexual availability. In this political climate, the "personal is political" is, arguably, taken too literally, and women's desire to either reject or embrace emotional intimacy is erroneously positioned as counterproductive to female agency.

Literary erotica

Sexuality is only one site of women's oppression and needs to be placed in context as such. To place too much emphasis on sexual desires and practices is to ignore the many other ways in which male domination is colluded with and resisted, and the many other means by which women's subordination is perpetuated and challenged. Even so, in this chapter, we have witnessed how bestselling, non-fiction erotic memoirs expose elements of both female empowerment and female oppression. Most strikingly, these accounts relay sexual ideologies and encounters in a forthright, distinctly non-literary style, marking a departure in the aesthetic and conceptual trajectory of literary erotica as defined by writers such as Pauline Reage. As popular texts produced for mainstream consumption, it is hardly surprising that they espouse conventional gender regimes framed in discourses of neo-liberal empowerment. If popular discourses in postfeminist culture do, as Yvonne Tasker argues, employ "playful strategies, both visual and narrative", to enact "a knowingness that ingeniously recommends conservative gender paths",[82] then should we expect literary erotica – a genre that "always entails a breaking down

DOI: 10.1057/9781137326546

of established patterns and of the regulated social order"[83] – to subvert prescriptive models of gendered behaviour and subjectivities?

The tradition of literary erotica has articulated sexual expression as a radical force, the erotic as a destructive but ultimately liberating energy that challenges the boundaries of social norms and etiquette. Georges Bataille's *Story of the Eye* (1928) delineates an integration of sex and violence, and is saturated with semen, urine, tears, egg yolks and cat's milk, while the author's writings on La Villette slaughterhouse are permeated with images of blood and unidentifiable bundles of visceral excess. Even his contemporary, Andre Breton, who was hardly a political reactionary, commented that "M.Bataille professes to wish only to consider in the world that which is vilest, most discouraging and most corrupted, so as to avoid making himself useful for anything specific."[84] Breton saw Bataille as the chief architect of a form of dissident surrealism that encouraged a descent into debauchery; Bataille's riposte was to highlight his work's recuperation of subversive desire as encouraging the transformation of matter into metaphor in an ascending movement of sublimation.

Toni Bentley's *The Surrender: An Erotic Memoir* is a 21st century extension of Bataille's aesthetic trajectory, with the author declaring "I came to know God experientially, from being fucked in the ass – over and over and over again."[85] Bentley's memoir explores the spiritual dimension of anal sex through physical and metaphysical contexts, which immediately places the text far from the mass-market memoirs of Lee, Townsend and Portnoy targeted at a mainstream audience. The text remains one of the few to actively situate its sexual politics in context of feminist writing and scholarship, and is written in a manner that is distinctly literary and – at least compared to mass-market erotic memoirs – highly sophisticated. It provides, therefore, a useful frame of reference for gauging the extent to which postfeminist culture has coopted and undermined the genre of literary erotica.

Yet, prior to exploring the extent to which Bentley's sexual ideologies and practices diverge from her mainstream counterparts, it is first important to explore the points where mass-market and literary memoirs converge, despite their substantial differences in style, subject and target audience. Certainly, in terms of sexual ideologies, Bentley's text shares affinities with the memoirs of Portnoy, Townsend and Lee. First, she condemns the "curious double standard" regarding the attitude of heterosexual men to anal sex: "How can they expect a woman to take a cock up her ass when they squeal if anything larger than a pinky finger is

DOI: 10.1057/9781137326546

waved in their direction?"[86] Like Townsend, we also witness Bentley ori-
enteering safe-sex practices in an uncompromising repudiation of sexual
encounters that are not mutually satisfying: "There were only two rules
that governed my behavior. One was relentlessly safe sex – I became the
Queen of Condoms. The second was the importance of quality control.
If the sex isn't awesome, or at least fascinating, get out, stop, shift gears,
and change direction with minimum discussion."[87] More prominently,
Bentley posits a rejection of heterosexual romantic love, marriage and
emotional intimacy, commenting that being a "Mrs" "felt horrendous",
while "Ms" represented a "dry, neutered alternative", concluding that the
"problem with them all is that what followed was always a man's name".[88]

This may seem to be a political stance that, in principle, ostensibly
rejects the commodification of female identity, yet the author's rejection
of monogamy actually originates from disappointing prior experiences
and a fear of emotional submission. The author "caught several men
desiring matrimony", "married the best of them" and "found misery to
spare".[89] Even prior to marriage, she suspected that the proposals "were
more about insecurities and jealousies than about love, more about tying
[her] down emotionally when [she] needed tying down physically".[90]
After marriage, she chooses a non-monogamous, sexual relationship
with a man she loves, aware that the exclusivity of monogamy requires
a form of emotional surrender, stating "I loved him too much. I was
too vulnerable to give myself entirely to him."[91] Instead, she rationalises
that, in the absence of "a commitment that might be broken", there is no
danger of the "self-righteous pain and anger of betrayal"[92] that infidelity
would precipitate. As such, she begins a relationship with "A-Man" that
never extends beyond the boundaries of non-monogamous anal sex,
choosing a sexual practice that the author situates as a feminist strategy:
"a pussy, genetically, wants impregnation, the juice; an asshole wants
the ride of its life".[93] For the author, she and her lover "exist in the land
beyond the intercourse that breeds babies".[94] Bentley's rejection of the
institution of marriage, monogamy, emotional intimacy and decentering
of vaginal intercourse all imply an affinity with the postfeminist ethos
disseminated in the memoirs of Townsend, Portnoy and Lee.

Yet, the reductionism of her comment that "vaginas are for babies,
asses for art"[95] subtly implicates her ideology as one grounded in the
rhetoric of biological essentialism, and we observe this further in her
adulation of heroic masculinity. Bentley admires that her lover had "the
balls to want and try and dare to fuck [her] in [her] tiny, tight ass",[96] and

DOI: 10.1057/9781137326546

audaciously positions second-wave feminism as culpable in the disintegration of normative masculinity: "Defusing the bomb is a challenge to the feminist man, and arrogance makes him think he can succeed. He can't. It's my hurt, my pain, and who are you to take it from me? I don't need rescuing, I don't need pity, I don't need opinions, I need fucking – and maybe a nice little spanking for indulging my anger."[97] The author does not require a man to attempt psychological understanding or emotional intimacy, but rather to uphold what she perceives to be his rightful place in the dominant sexual hierarchy. For a man to do any less than sexually dominate her positions him as an anomaly who can, in the 21st century, hide his deficiency under the cover of feminist enlightenment: "women's liberation has fostered what appears to be an entire generation of this particular man: the male masochist who can now masquerade, legitimately, as the feminist man."[98] Her resistance to the ideal of the enlightened, modern man ensures that, throughout the memoir, she assumes a subservient position in all her sexual interactions, first through acting as a vessel for learning and self-awareness: "I learned with him that I am most alive, most observant, and most intelligent when sexually engaged."[99] Ultimately, she finds sexual compatibility with a man who "was not going to compromise himself for pussy, like so many men do".[100]

It is Bentley's affirmation of sexual essentialism and narrowly defined gender roles that culminates in her positioning of male sexual behaviour as the preeminent marker of male identity: "If a man can possess a woman sexually – really possess – he won't need to control her ideas, her opinions, her clothes, her friends, even her other lovers."[101] The implication here is that male domination in all spheres of life is merely a compensation for a man's inability to assume a position of sexual dominance. Bentley suggests that male sexual dominance ensures that her lover has "infiltrated the core"[102] of her being, after which female submission in all other aspects of life is inevitable and legitimate. The author identifies the aftershock of feminist thought as a challenge to sexual empowerment, and positions her sexual pleasure in the convoluted territory between two polar opposites: "Domination – total and complete domination of my being – that is where I find freedom."[103] It is here that Bentley displays that she is an heir of the tradition of erotica developed by Reage and Bataille, by configuring sex as necessarily destructive and liberating, and by identifying feminism as an obstacle to relinquishing control and celebrating the "natural" order of sexual power structures: "He fucks me

DOI: 10.1057/9781137326546

into my femininity. As a liberated woman, it is the only way I can go there and retain my dignity. Turned over, ass in the air, I have little choice but to succumb and lose my head. This is how I can have an experience my intellect would never allow, a betrayal to Olive Schreiner, Margaret Sanger and Betty Friedan."[104]

This betrayal of a history of feminist struggle, both first and second-wave, and valorisation of sexual essentialism is distinctly postfeminist. Yvonne Tasker has highlighted postfeminism's "suppressed paradox of a simultaneous celebration of female empowerment and more traditional norms of femininity",[105] with reactionary gender regimes masked by a cosmetic subversion of traditional femininity. This is embodied in Bentley's declaration that, "Ass-fucking a woman is clearly about authority. The man's authority; the woman's complete acceptance of it."[106] By using the term "ass-fucking" – more commonly aligned with masculine expression and gonzo porn – Bentley subverts feminine scripts while affirming an essentialist discourse that remains as rigid as Freud's contention that male activity and female passivity is an unavoidable characteristic of sexual life.[107] In a further allusion to Freud, Bentley concedes to penis envy: "I reckon every woman wants a cock between her legs, ultimately. The question is: Does she want one of her own, or can she tolerate one belonging to a man?"[108] Her phallocentrism is so strong that she even declares that she "cannot love a cock that cannot dominate [her]", otherwise she retains "too much power" and becomes "totally tyrannical".[109] She resolutely positions women as desiring subordination, while simultaneously positioning herself as a liberated woman.

Along with Patrick Califia, the author can be identified as one among a minority of contemporary feminists who affirm sexual subordination. Califia locates this in the parameters of the wider feminist community by stating that "A woman who deliberately seeks out a sexual situation in which she can be helpless is a traitor in their eyes" largely because the women's movement has "been trying to persuade people for years that women are not naturally masochistic".[110] Yet, he also makes the astute point that subordination and masochism in the sexual realm does not necessarily represent power relations in the non-sexual sphere, either private or political: "A sexual masochist probably doesn't want to be raped, battered, discriminated against in her job, or kept down by the system. Her desire to act out a specific sexual fantasy is very different from the pseudopsychiatric dictum that a woman's world is bound by housework, intercourse, and childbirth."[111] By positing submission

DOI: 10.1057/9781137326546

in the locale of sexual relations, while maintaining control in other aspects of public and private life, Bentley thus complicates the divisive issue of whether or not sexual submission is indeed counterproductive to female agency, or indeed detrimental to women's experience in the wider social world. Even so, despite the ostensibly liberating ethos of *The Surrender*, it remains fair to suggest that the memoir is trapped within male-dominated sexual discourses that are limiting to women's sexual empowerment, if not their sexual pleasure. The distinction is an important one to make, for as Kathrina Glitre declares, "neoliberalism and the postfeminist sensibility encourage self-indulgent pleasure to be mistaken for empowerment".[112] While it is clear that Bentley experiences sexual pleasure as agentic, her pleasure is predicated on a strict adherence to the sexual paradigm of mainstream pornography – particularly the eroticisation of male power – in a manner that denies her material agency.

During the past 40 years, feminists have sought to radically change the manner in which sexual relations are played out between the sexes. They have sought to decentre penetration, to reconceptualise it in ways which do not position women as passive objects, and to change the manner in which women engage in sex with men. Feminists have argued that the possibility of empowerment for young women entails critical consideration of how women can respond to the pressures on them to treat sexual encounters as primarily for fulfilling men's sexual needs.[113] They have challenged the lack of a positive model of female sexuality, and argued that women must critically reflect on their sexual experiences in order to gain control of their responses to men. By questioning monogamy and supporting sexual freedom, writers associated with the women's movement in the 1960s and 1970s undoubtedly created a positive shift in the way that women perceived their sexuality, allowing women to discuss physical realities and lay claim to their own desires and pleasure.

In this chapter, I have aimed to illustrate how Lee, Portnoy, Townsend, and Bentley are heirs of this tradition of frank sexual discussion, and how their work demonstrates a plethora of (post)feminist sensibilities; the centralisation of women's desire for sex without emotional intimacy, the rejection of the codes of heterosexual romantic love, and the relegation of men to the sphere of sexual objects. All of this can be read as women's progress in the drive to invert inequalities in the male-dominated history of sexual relations. Yet, I have also aimed to illustrate how, despite the apparently liberating ethos of each of the memoirs, all are trapped within

DOI: 10.1057/9781137326546

male-dominated discourses that are limiting to women's sexual freedom; not merely in their saturation and acceptance of the values of the sex industry, but most importantly, in their eroticisation of male power and self-objectification. The memoirs demonstrate that even when women are powerfully vocalising their sexual preferences and aspirations, many of these desires remain unrealised in the context of real-world sexual encounters. The memoirs suggest that while it is very easy for 21st century women to express their sexual desires, it is infinitely more difficult to specify what, exactly, is meant by empowerment in sexual relations when women are subordinate to men.

Notes

1   Stevi Jackson, "Heterosexuality, Power and Pleasure" in *Feminism and Sexuality: A Reader*, eds Stevi Jackson and Sue Scott (Edinburgh: Edinburgh University Press, 1996), 175–180.

2   Sarah Gamble, "Postfeminism" in *The Routledge Companion to Feminism and Postfeminism*, ed. Sarah Gamble (London and New York: Routledge, 1998), 43.

3   Ibid.

4   Ibid., 44.

5   Ibid.

6   Natasha Walter, *Living Dolls: The Return of Sexism* (London: Virago, 2010), 68.

7   Ibid., 49.

8   Gamble, "Postfeminism", 44.

9   Ibid.

10   Natasha Walter, *The New Feminism* (London: Virago, 1999), 112.

11   Ibid., 113.

12   Ibid., 112.

13   Suzanne Portnoy, *The Butcher, the Baker, the Candlestick Maker* (London: Virgin Books, 2006), 85.

14   Ibid., 1.

15   Ibid., 2.

16   Ibid., 9.

17   Ibid., 41.

18   Abby Lee, *Girl with a One Track Mind: Confessions of the Seductress Next Door* (London: Ebury Press, 2006), 105.

19   Ibid., 104–105.

20   Catherine Townsend, *Sleeping Around: Secrets of a Sexual Adventuress* (London: John Murray, 2007), 3.

21   Ibid., 86.

DOI: 10.1057/9781137326546

22 Robert Jensen, *Getting Off: Pornography and the End of Masculinity* (Cambridge, MA: South End Press, 2007), 158.
23 Townsend, *Sleeping Around*, 57–58.
24 Walter, *The New Feminism*, 120.
25 Lee, *Girl with a One Track Mind*, vii.
26 While mainstream television programmes such as *Sex in the City* celebrate female sexual expression and autonomy, all of its female characters ultimately pursue a life partner.
27 Lee, *Girl with a One Track Mind*, viii.
28 Ibid., viii–ix.
29 Walter, *The New Feminism*, 106.
30 Portnoy, *The Butcher*, 25.
31 Ibid., 17.
32 Ibid., 25.
33 Ibid.
34 Ibid., 144.
35 Ibid., 113.
36 Townsend, *Sleeping Around*, 166.
37 Ibid., 4–5.
38 Ibid., 185.
39 Lee, *Girl with a One Track Mind*, viii.
40 Janet Holland, Caroline Ramazanoglu, Sue Sharpe and Rachel Thomson, "Pressured Pleasure: Young Women and the Negotiation of Sexual Boundaries" in *Feminism and Sexuality: A Reader*, eds Stevi Jackson and Sue Scott (Edinburgh: Edinburgh University Press, 1996), 258.
41 Ibid., 249.
42 Ibid., 251.
43 Portnoy, *The Butcher*, 10.
44 Townsend, *Sleeping Around*, 59.
45 Portnoy, *The Butcher*, 68.
46 Townsend, *Sleeping Around*, 85.
47 Ibid.
48 Lee, *Girl with a One Track Mind*, 12.
49 Portnoy, *The Butcher*, 69.
50 Ibid., 23.
51 Ibid., 93.
52 Ibid., 69.
53 Holland *et al.*, "Pressured Pleasure", 252.
54 Portnoy, *The Butcher*, 42.
55 Lee, *Girl with a One Track Mind*, 165.
56 Ibid.
57 Walter, *The New Feminism*, 120.

DOI: 10.1057/9781137326546

58   Previously Pat, now Patrick Califia after undergoing gender reassignment.

59   Pat Califia, "Feminism and Sadomasochism" in *Feminism and Sexuality: A Reader*, eds Stevi Jackson and Sue Scott (Edinburgh: Edinburgh University Press, 1996), 232.

60   Townsend, *Sleeping Around*, 62.

61   Lynne Segal, *Straight Sex: The Politics of Pleasure* (London: Virago, 1994), 45.

62   Walter, *Living Dolls*, 105.

63   Townsend, *Sleeping Around*, 135.

64   Since the ascent of the Internet, the vast majority of Western teenagers' first sexual experience is witnessing strangers performing sexual intercourse. 'Performance' is indeed the vital word, as many young women today are unconsciously coerced into constructing a self-limiting version of desire by imitating actresses in pornography who are themselves imitating sexual desire.

65   Townsend, *Sleeping Around*, 98.

66   Portnoy, *The Butcher*, 142.

67   Ibid., 132.

68   Townsend, *Sleeping Around*, 72.

69   Portnoy, *The Butcher*, 118.

70   Ibid., 112.

71   Ibid., 13.

72   Ibid.

73   Ibid.

74   Ibid., 14.

75   Townsend, *Sleeping Around*, 71–72.

76   Portnoy, *The Butcher*, 207.

77   Ibid., 208.

78   Ibid., 218.

79   Lee, *Girl with a One Track Mind*, 309.

80   Townsend, *Sleeping Around*, 274.

81   Ibid.

82   Yvonne Tasker, "*Enchanted* (2007) by Postfeminism: Gender, Irony and the New Romantic Comedy" in *Feminism at the Movies: Understanding Gender in Contemporary Popular Cinema*, eds Hilary Radner and Rebecca Stringer (London and New York: Routledge, 2011), 70.

83   Georges Bataille, *Eroticism*, trans. M. Dalwood (London: Penguin, 2001 [1954]), 8.

84   Andre Breton, *Manifestoes of Surrealism*, trans. R. Seaver and H.R. Lane (Ann Arbor: University of Michigan Press, 1998 [1924]), 234.

85   Toni Bentley, *The Surrender: An Erotic Memoir* (London: Harper Perennial, 2006), 4.

86   Ibid., 115.

DOI: 10.1057/9781137326546

87   Ibid., 34.
88   Ibid., 204.
89   Ibid., 76.
90   Ibid.
91   Ibid., 176.
92   Ibid.
93   Ibid., 186.
94   Ibid., 83.
95   Ibid., 126.
96   Ibid., 78.
97   Ibid., 137.
98   Ibid., 49.
99   Ibid., 31.
100 Ibid., 176.
101 Ibid., 98.
102 Ibid.
103 Ibid.
104 Ibid., 7.
105 Tasker, *Enchanted*, 70.
106 Ibid., 91.
107 See Sigmund Freud, "The Sexual Aberrations" in *Three Essays on the Theory of Sexuality*, trans. James Strachey (New York: Basic Books, 1987), 24.
108 Bentley, *The Surrender*, 42.
109 Ibid., 128.
110 Califia, "Feminism and Sadomasochism", 234.
111 Ibid., 235.
112 Kathrina Glitre, "Nancy Meyers and Popular Feminism" in *Women on Screen: Feminism and Femininity in Visual Culture*, ed. Melanie Waters (Basingstoke: Palgrave Macmillan, 2011), 28.
113 Holland *et al.*, "Pressured Pleasure", 1996.

DOI: 10.1057/9781137326546

2
Intimacy

Abstract: *This chapter focuses on the relationship between postfeminist culture and the mainstreaming of the sex industry, paying particular attention to new constructions of sexual intimacy in the 21st century. It seeks to determine if women's erotic memoirs locate sexual intimacy as predicated on traditional scripts of love and romance, or if postfeminist "raunch culture" has entirely coopted feminist resistance to traditional relationships by positioning sexual promiscuity as a legitimate mode of empowerment. It pursues this line of enquiry by demonstrating how women's erotic memoirs position commercial and non-commercial sexual encounters in close proximity, as experiences where emotional and physical intimacies are similarly produced and consumed.*

Gwynne, Joel. *Erotic Memoirs and Postfeminism: The Politics of Pleasure.* Basingstoke: Palgrave Macmillan, 2013.
DOI: 10.1057/9781137326546.

DOI: 10.1057/9781137326546

The form of the memoir is inherently intimate, and popular women's memoirs function in counterpoint to public narratives of sexuality which largely focus on behaviour and attitudes confined to the realms of gendered social acceptability. The memoir is, therefore, highly private, with narrative voices often claiming to relay experiences that are entirely genuine, predominantly confessional and frequently controversial. We only have to recall the media storm surrounding James Frey's *A Million Little Pieces* (2003) to remind ourselves that memoirs are often consciously fictionalised or unconsciously unreliable, but even so, it is the very nature of perceived authenticity on the part of the reader that establishes the memoir as a subjective, yet undeniably intimate genre. Memoirs often present narratives in the form of diary entries, and the intrinsic intimacy of this mode is enhanced even further when erotic content is introduced, consistent with the status of sex as the most taboo form of intimacy. In the erotic memoir, the reader occupies a surreptitious and voyeuristic space, and the intimate relationship between audience and author is further enhanced by the disclosure of sex as a site of not only pleasure, but also uncomfortable and transgressive experiences.

Robert Jensen comments that "precisely because they are powerful experiences, intimacy and sex are never risk free", and continues to assert that "attempts to make this human interaction free of any risk would almost certainly render human interaction meaningless".[1] Naomi Wolf makes a similar point, charting the memoir as the preserve of transgressive stories, of narratives which "are rarely spoken outside that private space, or after adolescence, because they include elements of sex and greed, danger and narcissism, insecurity and bad behaviour".[2] These private stories, especially stories of female promiscuity, are indeed private as they often directly subvert or subtly reconfigure mainstream public narratives of sex which, according to Lynne Jamieson, "offer a variety of contradictory messages which sustain both a strong narrative of predatory male sexuality separated from intimacy and a romantic fusion of sex and intimacy".[3] Jamieson continues to observe that while it is impossible to definitively judge the balance of narratives within popular culture, films, advertising, television shows, novels and the like, "predatory male sexuality remains a celebrated theme and a commercially successful formula",[4] one which, I contend, is often disrupted by popular women's memoirs.

Narratives of female desire are relegated to the private sphere largely due to limited public space for their expression, despite the fact that

DOI: 10.1057/9781137326546

the 21st century bears witness to a diverse and increasing range of sexual economies and practices represented in the mainstream media. Contemporary Western societies, most notably the US and UK, have become increasingly hypersexual, and postmillennial Britain has been described by Natasha Walter as not only "a new culture of shags and threesomes, orgies and stranger fucks", but more importantly a hyper-sexual culture that "seems to be replacing the culture in which sex was associated with the flowering of intimacy".[5] Constructions of intimacy have undeniably shifted over the past decade, but what media represen-tations of sexual expression do not reveal is the intricate and divisive relationship between physical and emotional forms of intimacy. There is substantial evidence which suggests a widespread acceptance of the merits of parity in sexual relationships, emerging from a more widely documented acceptance of the egalitarian relationship as a measure by which increasing numbers of people feel they must judge their own indi-vidual lives. Jeffrey Weeks has observed that "At the centre of this ideal is the fundamental belief that love relationships and partnerships should be a matter not of arrangement or tradition, but of personal choice based on a balance of attraction, desire, mutual trust and compatibility."[6] Yet, despite this optimistic assessment, Anthony Giddens has argued that the late 20th century is also characterised by an addiction to sex and damaging relationships, claiming that tradition has been thoroughly swept away leaving individuals vulnerable to being overwhelmed by choice in romantic and sexual relationships.[7] In postfeminist culture, the potentially detrimental effects of the rise in sexual exchanges without emotional intimacy or long-term commitment are often underplayed, and cited as evidence of modern women's freedom of sexual expression. Postfeminist promiscuity is packaged as liberating, a long-awaited anti-dote to the social reality that, for most of the 20th century, "men have been portrayed as pursuing and being enhanced by sexual adventures which split sex from love and intimacy, while women are presented as degraded by such exploits."[8]

Popular women's memoirs suggest that, in the 21st century, women taking the initiative in love and sex has become a more common cul-tural theme in accordance with a more expansive dissolution of the bond between emotional and sexual intimacy. What is perhaps most striking, however, is the role that new global technologies, such as the expansion of the Internet and mobile communications, have played in reconfiguring how intimate relationships develop. Similarly, the

DOI: 10.1057/9781137326546

increasing sexualisation of Western cultures is often linked to the growth of the sex industry through new communications and technologies, and the impact of the mainstreaming of the porn industry is discernible in the expansion of commercial-sex services. Publishing industries have mirrored this expansion, and memoirs of prostitution are among the genre's most popular. While this cultural movement is hardly surprising, what is unexpected is the extent to which contemporary memoirs position commercial sex and non-commercial promiscuity as sites for the exchange of new forms of intimacy and social transmission. This is interesting because, as Teela Sanders has observed, "commentators on intimacy have not considered commercial sex as a site where intimacy is sought or exchanged", largely because the "primacy of the sexual aspects of the relationship have been privileged over any complex understanding of the sex worker-client relationship".[9]

In this chapter, I aim to answer the following questions: How do contemporary women's memoirs construct intimacy in the 21st century? To what extent is sexual intimacy still governed by traditional notions of love and romance? How has the mainstreaming of the sex industry affected constructions of intimacy? How has the Internet and new communication technologies reconfigured constructions of intimacy? And finally, to what extent do contemporary erotic memoirs position commercial and non-commercial sexual relationships in close proximity, as sites where emotional and physical intimacies are similarly produced and consumed?

Intimacy and pleasure

Jeffrey Weeks has commented that the strong emotions that sexual exchanges arouse present to the world of sexuality "a seismic sensitivity making it a transmission belt for a wide variety of needs and desires", locating sex as an experience that convenes "love and anger, tenderness and aggression, intimacy and adventure, romance and predatoriness, pleasure and pain, empathy and power".[10] Sexuality is understood subjectively, and while traditional romantic narratives present sex as the culmination of flowering emotional intimacy between two parties, there has been very little research conducted on role of sex in the development of love. This is perhaps due to the fact that sex education has historically focused on the biological and reproductive aspects of sex, with the

DOI: 10.1057/9781137326546

emotional dimensions and the physiology of sexual pleasure relegated to the margins. Likewise, Shere Hite has charted the negative effects of a history of public silence on the experience of female sexual pleasure. In a survey conducted on samples of adult men and women, Hite discovered that while 60 per cent of the male sample confessed to group masturbation in adolescence, women had typically not taken part in this activity, reporting that girlhood masturbation exists predominantly as a solitary, private and guilty secret.[11]

Lynne Jamieson has also noted the detrimental implications of this culture of silence, especially the negative effects of women's inability to express their sexual preferences on emotional intimacy: "The consequence for women is both less satisfactory sex and feeling less loved, a loss of intimacy which feeds back into less satisfactory sex."[12] It is, however, not solely women who suffer from an inability to communicate their expectations, hopes and fears surrounding sexual exchanges. Men, too, are frequently isolated by limiting discourses of sexuality, and Harry Brod contends that "a confession that sex is vastly overrated often lies beneath male sexual bravado." Brod suggests that "sex seems overrated because men look to sex for the fulfilment of nonsexual emotional needs", a quest "doomed to failure" due to the "priority of quantity over quality of sex which comes with sexuality's commodification".[13] If women are pressured to remain silent where sexual desire and activity is concerned, then men are similarly pressured to associate emotional intimacy primarily, if not exclusively, in the context of sexual conquest.

Even though this gender distinction may remain true today, even within postfeminist culture, there is no doubt that contemporary sexologists identify sex as central to the development of emotional intimacy. Jamieson observes that "Sex, love and intimacy are analytically separate but in social practices they are often linked, as the phrase 'making love' illustrates", and affirms the role of sex as a culmination of the process of falling in love: "If the way in which people learn to feel sexy (when and with whom they want to have sex) is structured by a popular story of 'falling-in-love', then sex is linked to love in the construction of their sexuality."[14] Yet, what sexologists and the media rarely discuss, and what popular women's memoirs resolutely demonstrate, is the inverse of this common pattern: feelings of emotional intimacy developing as a culmination of, and dependant on, satisfactory sexual exchanges. Toni Bentley's *The Surrender* (2006) aggressively asserts this notion, with the author declaring: "I fell madly, quickly, and completely, forever, the first

DOI: 10.1057/9781137326546

time he fucked my ass. Now it's #220 and my love has only deepened – 220 times deeper."[15]

For Bentley, satisfactory sexual intercourse is essential to falling in love, and sexual sacrifice is essential to expressing love, even if it involves physical pain: "Gagging is good. If you won't gag for your man, how can you really love him?"[16] Melissa P.'s *One Hundred Strokes of the Brush Before Bed* (2004) presents a similar notion, with the protagonist confessing: "I know that all I need to do is make love with the Prof one last time to be sure of what I really want and what Melissa really is, whether a monster or someone who is truly capable of giving and receiving love."[17] Yet, unlike Bentley, who identifies sexual pleasure as a precursor to the development of love, Melissa P. remains bound in romantic ideologies that construct sex as interdependent with love and the flowering of intimacy: "I believed that in the long run even a porno novel might metamorphose into a tale of love and affection, which, absent at the start, could develop with practice."[18] At a later point in the memoir, she expresses this sentiment again after a sexual encounter, reflecting on "a passion that wasn't sexual desire, but a yearning for something else, for love".[19]

For Melissa P. sex is, therefore, positioned as a necessary step on the road to complete emotional intimacy, a form of currency that can be exchanged to ensure the successful purchase of love. Abby Lee's *Girl with a One Track Mind* (2006) mirrors this position, with the author commenting that, "Getting the sex stuff out of the way helped us become much closer, and we can now talk very honestly about sex, which is wonderful."[20] Lee confesses the importance of sexual intimacy in a rather apologetic manner, stating that: "It's not that I fetishise the cock over the man: I am learning that my attraction to a guy is more about his personality, intelligence and attitude," yet continues to claim that she becomes "more intimate with [her lover] by striking up a relationship with his cock".[21] The term "relationship" is revealing, suggesting that Lee perceives the penis as not simply a part of a man's anatomy, but as an extension of her lover's emotional and psychological selfhood. Contemporary erotic memoirs are, therefore, often extreme in their reconfiguration of traditional constructions of the development of love by suggesting that understanding a lover's physicality is an essential step to understanding the emotional and psychological aspects of character.

Catherine Millet's *The Sexual Life of Catherine M.* presents to the reader an explanation of why so many memoirs centralise the role of sex in the development of emotional intimacy: "In fact, I only really relaxed

DOI: 10.1057/9781137326546

once I had removed my dress or my trousers. My true clothing was my nudity, which shielded me."²² The identification of the body as one of the preeminent sources of identity is discussed in great detail throughout the text, with the author proclaiming that to establish a relationship one must "negotiate an exchange of words or at least signals, the sort of complicity which forms the basis of all conversations". Millet sees this process as "closely related to the preliminaries of seduction" for one must "take into account your partner's attitudes and responses". Upon this realisation, she prioritises engagement with the body as the first and most important step to developing an intimate relationship: "Now, even at the first contact, I knew only how to focus on the body." Only after Millet has "found [her] bearings with the body" to the extent that "the grain of the skin and its particular pigmentation have become familiar" can she turn her attention to "focus onto the person themselves".²³

Similarly, in Melissa P's *One Hundred Strokes of the Brush Before Bed* the narrator only begins to love her partner after she has imprinted herself onto his body. After a night of sex during which her body is "saturated with such euphoria," and "becalmed by a sensation of utter bliss" which "engulfs [her] completely", Melissa learns that "letting yourself go with someone you like, someone who overwhelms your senses, is a sacred thing", and something more than simply a physical exchange: "It's then that sex ceases to be merely sex and begins to be love, while nuzzling the scented skin on his back or caressing his strong, soft shoulders or smoothing his hair."²⁴ Throughout the memoir, Melissa sees the body as the means of communing with matters of the heart, declaring that she will "give [her] body to any man who comes along, for two reasons", first so that in "savouring [her] he might taste [her] rage and bitterness and therefore experience a modicum of tenderness" and second so that "he might fall so deeply in love with [her] passion that he won't be able to do without it".²⁵ The use of the word "passion" here is interesting, and it is clear that Melissa positions "passion" as both an expression of the body and of the soul. Taken quite literally, on a purely sexual level, falling in love with passion could simply equate to being enraptured by the tactile experience of bodily connection. However, the expression also encompasses falling in love with the passion of the soul, the "rage and bitterness" that can only be transmitted through sexual exchange. Melissa P's memoir suggests, then, that it is only through sexual intercourse that the core of a variety of human experiences can be accessed, especially those which transmit pain and vulnerability.

DOI: 10.1057/9781137326546

This is especially clear in Bentley's *The Surrender*, which configures sex as a way of rearticulating childhood trauma through emotional sublimation. The narrator describes her lover's penis as "pressing into [her] anxieties, [her] pettiness, [her] pride, [her] vanity", a psychological as much as physical penetration in which the phallus expunges "lesser selves" and locates "[her] goodness, [her] innocence, [her] four-year-old before she was hit by The Hand".[26] As we should perhaps expect with Bentley, the passage possesses anti-feminist implications, suggesting that it is only through sexual submission that her "goodness" can be found, a purity that is entirely dependent on a submissive sexuality that reconciles her adult self with the innocence of her pre-abused childhood state. After Bentley "suck[s] his cock more fabulously than ever before, that much deeper, that much slower, that much faster", her lover "takes [her] head firmly in his hands, refocuses, looks [her] straight in the eye and says, 'Good girl.'". The effect on Bentley is dramatic: "To think I've been through all this, come this far, just to find out that all I ever really wanted was to be a good girl, Daddy's good girl. Finally."[27]

Aside from the conspicuous paedophilic subtext, Bentley's memoir understands sex as a means of reclaiming a loss of intimacy in childhood, a characteristic which greatly improves the quality of sex experienced in the exchange. The fact that pleasurable sexual exchanges are defined by a movement between an absence of emotional intimacy (in Bentley's childhood experience) and an abundance of emotional intimacy (in her adult relationship) is a dominant pattern across a number of memoirs. In pronouncing the latter, Bentley confesses that she is "surprised at how much [she] liked sucking [her lover's] cock", rationalising that this is "because he had shown [her] love first, and filled with gratitude, [she] headed down".[28] The memoirs of Townsend and Lee make similar claims, with the former conceding that, despite her current lifestyle of casual sex, the "hottest sex ever was with JP, because we were in love and I felt really comfortable".[29]

Lee, approaching this subject from the opposite perspective, laments the poor quality of sex experienced in the absence of emotional intimacy: "I had sex with men that not only didn't give a shit about me, but actually pretended to give a shit about me in order to get me into bed [...] Sex with these men was dreadful, without exception."[30] Yet, despite the onus that all of these memoirs place on the affirmative role of emotional intimacy in sexual encounters, many chart the territory that Bentley explores in her description of enjoyable intercourse; as predicated on convening

DOI: 10.1057/9781137326546

both emotional closeness and emotional distance. Even though this is, in Bentley's case, articulated as a summoning of a previously submerged childhood trauma, she also locates this conflict between distance and closeness in more immediate and apparent terms. She announces the importance of emotional insecurity in achieving satisfactory sex, a state that forces both parties to "constantly confront the spaces" between them. Bentley's lover "never overstays his welcome" and "cultivates an air of scarcity", creating "an erotic component of powerful and paradoxical consequences".[31] It is precisely this "element of instability", rather than emotional closeness and security, that generates "the total thrill of each and every encounter", for the "lost heat that monogamous couples constantly mourn is always there"[32] due to the unpredictability and potential intransience of the emotional bond.

As Bentley is not committed to a relationship bound by the principles of monogamy and frequent contact, the tactile experience of bodily pleasure is not rendered habitual and emotional bonds remain precarious. Townsend's *Breaking the Rules: Confessions of a Bad Girl* (2008) maps similar territory in its perspective on the appeal of role-play and the pretence of unfamiliarity in sexual encounters, constructing the practice as more than simply a "fun way to spice up a relationship". However, unlike Bentley, who more explicitly rejects conventional romance, Townsend is conflicted between enjoying the experience of sexual role play while feeling guilty about "trying to avoid intimacy", and even lamenting "I didn't want to have to get into character every time I got into bed".[33] At a later point in the memoir, Townsend again affirms the potency of a one-time sexual encounter that she describes as "way too intense for never-to-be-repeated sex" and rationalises that the absence of emotional intimacy was precisely why the encounter was so electrifying. In a statement that registers the contentious status of female sexual activity in society, Townsend comments that it is "sometimes easier to tell strangers our most intimate secrets", and "less difficult to make strange requests with someone you'll never see again".[34]

Bearing in mind Lynne Segal's observation that "a host of sanctions and constraints – legal, social and ideological – surrounds every aspect of women's sexuality",[35] it is hardly surprising that expressions of female sexual desire are most easily accomplished when emotional intimacy is absent and there is no risk of recrimination and judgement. While the memoirs discussed imply that emotional intimacy has no role of good sex, Krissy Kneen's *Affection: An Erotic Memoir* (2010) articulates

DOI: 10.1057/9781137326546

a movement between emotional intimacy and emotional distance, one that summons the necessary violence of passionate encounters that invoke past emotional residue: "The sex we had that night was not the comforting kind that we had grown used to. We stole pieces off each other, samples of skin secreted away under our fingernails, the taste of sweat, the bitter burn of his semen that I would taste at the back of my throat for days." In this encounter the lovers "didn't speak of the bad times, but they were there" in the "ruin of our relationship and the glory of our sex".[36] The memoir depicts enjoyable sex as a culmination of love and hate, where lovers are not emotionally distant but where emotional proximity is saturated with the memories of negative, as much as positive shared experiences.

Intimacy and hookup sex

The first chapter of this book focused on the dangers of identifying sexual assertion as a form of empowered female subjectivity, however I will now turn my attention to how women's erotic memoirs bear witness to the prioritisation of bodily pleasure over emotional fulfilment. As many feminists have already noted, the popularisation of sexual pleasure as a new form of feminist and feminine subjectivity can be tied to the mainstreaming of the ethics and aesthetics of porn (McRobbie 2009). The ethos at the heart of this cultural movement – the idea that sexual pleasure is by and of itself empowering – is remarkably concordant with the manner in which all forms of self-pleasure are accentuated in post-feminist culture as political treatise in their own right. Kathrina Glitre makes the observation that "Neoliberalism and the postfeminist sensibility encourage self-indulgent pleasure to be mistaken for empowerment, as if the mere fact that a woman enjoys doing something then this pleasure is, in some sense, 'feminist'."[37] This argument is often deployed by those who position pornography as empowering for women, yet scarce thought is given to how porn inevitably benefits men more than women. As Dines points out, in societies where the relationship between emotional intimacy and masculinity is inscribed in predominantly sexual terms, the emotional economy of pornography is appealing as it offers "a no-strings-attached, intense, disconnected sexual experience, where men always get to have as much sex as they want in ways that shore up their masculinity".

DOI: 10.1057/9781137326546

In the pornography paradigm of sexual relations, sex acts are "always successful, ending in supposed orgasm for both" and men are protected from rejection or ridicule since "women never say no to men's sexual demands, nor do they question their penis size or technique".[38] The role of pornography in the fortification of the male ego is premised not merely on its purpose as a form that serves to primarily enable male consumers to achieve orgasm, but also on the absence of emotional intimacy in porn exchanges. As porn performers are indeed performing sexuality, and therefore have no emotional investment in neither the sexual encounter nor in each other, porn sex is dehumanised. Natasha Walter has observed that in the porn paradigm there is "no before and no after" as sex occurs in isolation; no individuality as every partner is interchangeable; and no communication between the individuals concerned as all performance is directed at the observer.

According to Walter, the dehumanisation of sex at the hands of pornography has, to those who become imaginatively involved in its consumption, "real effects on their own relationships".[39] Whether due to the endemic mainstreaming of the sex industry and the sexualisation of Western cultures, widely documented in both popular journalism (Walter 2010, Levy 2006, Banyard 2010) and academic research (Gill 2006, Attwood 2009), or merely a consequence of the fallout of second-wave feminist thought that implicated romance narratives as prohibitive to female sexual activity outside of monogamous heterosexual relationships, there is little doubt that many memoirs position emotional intimacy as irrelevant to positive sexual encounters. Natasha Walter's evaluation of the contemporary sexual climate as one in which "for women who are not married, having many sexual partners without much emotional commitment is often seen as the most authentic way to behave",[40] testifies to the popularisation of the porn view of sexual exchange; that the "core reality of sex – what really matters – is that it's about physical pleasure".[41]

Kneen's *Affection* upholds this belief most distinctly in a conversation between the author and her psychotherapist: "Sex is clean. Easy. Sex has nothing to do with intimacy." Despite her awareness that "other people would disagree", including her psychotherapist, Kneen is "certain that sex and intimacy are completely separate in the scheme of things".[42] This sensibility is ubiquitous in contemporary memoirs, as is what Gail Dines refers to as "hookup" sex, "one of the most noticeable shifts in girls' and young women's behavior over the last decade".[43] Defining "hookup" sex

DOI: 10.1057/9781137326546

as encounters "that can be anything from a grope to full sexual inter-course but have the common feature that there is no expectation of a relationship, intimacy, or connection", Dines traces the link between this relatively new cultural phenomenon and porn sex: "Given its lack of commitment and intimate connection, hookup sex is a lot like porn sex, and it is being played out in the real world."[44] What Dines fails to explain persuasively, however, is why this trend poses a problem. If women experience "hookup" sex as pleasurable, then what concerns does this apparently new phenomenon raise? There remains, perhaps, the presence of a moral panic in Dines' argument surrounding "hookup" sex, and popular memoirs do not reveal promiscuity as a pattern of behaviour that is detrimental to female selfhood.

Documenting such cultural reverberations in real-world encounters, Dawn Porter's *Diaries of an Internet Lover* (2006) locates the growth of the Internet and new communication technologies as a facilitating mecha-nism for hookup sex. The narrator discusses the purpose of an unnamed website with a section titled *Casual Encounters,* as found on websites such as *Craigslist* and *Locanto*, "specifically designed for people who are looking for one off meetings with strangers" for "discreet, random and totally no-strings-attached sex".[45] The website provides the means for the narrator to "satisfy [her] passion for all things fruity" through meeting people who are "totally disconnected from [her] life".[46] The narrator self-describes as the "type of person who has slept with most of her friends",[47] demonstrating the fragile bonds of intimacy in a culture in which the sexual contract is no longer a marker of emotional exclusivity.

In a similar manner, even though Belle de Jour's *Intimate Adventures of a London Call Girl* (2005) predominantly documents her experience as a social escort, the text offers an insight into how intimacy within non-commercial exchanges often mirror commercial transactions. The narrator's description of unpaid casual sex with a stranger is revealing: "There wasn't much conversation. I didn't know what to say. Thank you, that was luscious, you know we're not going to see each other again, don't you?"[48] Likewise, in her own description of unpaid sex in her per-sonal life, the prostitute-narrator of Jenny Angell's *Callgirl* (2007) makes a similar point, celebrating that fact that "Fortunately, you don't have to speak to your partner in order to have sex."[49] This affirmation of the purposelessness of communication during intercourse is rationalised in Almudena Grandes' *The Ages of Lulu* (1993), with the author comment-ing that communication is unnecessary because "fucking in itself, hasn't

DOI: 10.1057/9781137326546

necessarily got anything to do with love".[50] Similarly, Townsend declares that "emotional intimacy and physical intimacy are two completely different animals",[51] while Bentley positions emotional intimacy as destructive to sexual desire: "I am well aware by now that if a man exhibits too many signs of attachment I lose interest and the sex becomes laden with obligation. Desire is sexy, a show of free will; attachment is the enemy of free will."[52]

In a similar vein, Bentley's rejection of the necessity of emotional intimacy in sexual encounters is motivated by an awareness and similar rejection of the pathologisation of female promiscuity: "About anonymity and sex. I find it very shortsighted to dismiss the concept of 'anonymous' sex – real or imagined – as 'impersonal' and shamefully indicative of one's unresolved intimacy issues."[53] Likewise, and in both of her memoirs, Townsend challenges the desirability of emotional intimacy in sexual encounters, and confesses that to "avoid embarrassing mishaps during introductions (and crying out the wrong name in the heat of passion), [she] long ago mastered the art of calling every guy sweetheart and honey".[54] Even though she "always maintained that the brain is the sexiest muscle for seduction" she later discovers that "a perfect set of abs seemed to be doing the trick" in arousing her, despite not knowing anything about her lover, including "what genre of movie he liked, his views on politics or even his middle name". Townsend supports both Bentley's view of sexual exchange and Dines' comments on the prolificacy of "hookup" sex by declaring that emotional intimacy is irrelevant as she can "write volumes on how he liked his neck kissed" and "how tightly [she] could bind him to his bed's headboard without causing wrist abrasions".[55] Suzanne Portnoy shares Townsend's perspective, commenting that on her "list of priorities, the cock came first. Face and bod were next, followed by brains and personality",[56] while Lee embraces the opportunity "to have some casual sex and skip the whole drama of meeting, chatting and getting to know someone".[57]

Yet, despite the attempts of contemporary women to circumnavigate the complexities of emotional intimacy in sexual relations, many find that, as Jensen mentioned earlier, "intimacy and sex are never risk free". Lee's memoir shows that even though the postfeminist woman may intend to enter into a purely sexual relationship without emotional attachment, the male lover can, of course, desire the opposite, leading to confusion and miscommunication. In the morning after an encounter which Lee understood as mutually casual, the author explains why she

DOI: 10.1057/9781137326546

chooses to suspend all postsex contact: "I didn't call you because when we woke up, you smiled at me, and pulled me close, and stroked my hair. And when you looked in my eyes, I saw a longing that terrified me." Lee realises that through the course of only one night, in an encounter described as "affectionate and caring and loving", she became "the replacement for [his] ex".[58] She realises that even when *she* expects an encounter to be purely sexual, it is easy for the exchange to become a point of emotional investment, if only for one party, largely because men still expect that women who begin a sexual relationship will ultimately desire a complete relationship. The memoirs of both Angell and Portnoy also acknowledge the dangers of possessing unrealistic expectations, with the former lamenting the sudden realisation "midway through [sex] that perhaps you don't really like this person all that much after all"[59] and the latter that "You can never be sure if you've read a new partner right or touched his body the way he really likes it touched."[60] These examples demonstrate that unexpected emotional and physical responses often colonise the casual-sex experience, and the memoirs suggest that while contemporary women are casting off social restrictions and engaging in encounters that are often fulfilling, it is nevertheless difficult to successfully navigate the intimate space that mediates where emotional and physical experiences converge.

Intimacy and internet dating

The sexualisation of Western cultures has principally been attributed to the mainstreaming of the sex industry, which has in turn been linked to the proliferation of sexual content and services in cyberspace. Teela Sanders has observed that virtual spaces have not only "become a marketplace for sex industries, particularly entrepreneurial sex work", but also a "meeting place for men who buy sex to express and form their sexual and personal identities".[61] Sanders' research is concerned with how the Internet operates in men's negotiation of and access to experiences of intimacy, identity and networks. She is particularly interested in male sexual storytelling, especially in the context of the "field report", which she defines as "textual narratives of sexual selves and evidence of the proliferation of personal narratives"[62] of sexuality which have found both a voice and an audience in cyberspace. In these narratives, in which clients review and evaluate their experiences with sex workers, "men

DOI: 10.1057/9781137326546

express their masculinity and reflections on their own sexual perform-ance through self-constructed narratives of their sexual encounters". In accordance with the social acceptability of male narratives of sexuality, these "field reports" are easily found online, and are public perform-ances of intimate sex acts that "promote self-narratives of the sexual performance through a medium that is open for all to read". Women's erotic memoirs are, therefore, strikingly concordant with male-authored "field reports", for both present private experiences as public narratives/ performances and demonstrate, in very different ways, that computer-mediated communication and cybercultures are dramatically changing both constructions of intimacy and the nature of social relationships.

Indeed, Sanders' description of the "field report" reveals striking cor-relations between the documentation of sexual encounters written by men and sexual encounters written by women:

> The impression given is that the sexual account is of a 'real'-life encounter between the writer and a sex worker. There is obviously no way of knowing if these accounts ever took place, and even if they did, the report represents an interpretation of events by one actor, at a certain time and place, with a specific audience in mind and reputation to maintain.[63]

If we remove the term "sex worker" from the evaluation and replace it with "lover", then the statement could quite easily be a description of the erotic memoir, as both forms call into question notions of authenticity, representation and audience reception. Similarly, if in Sanders' under-standing "field reports" function as not merely vehicles of voyeuristic sexual gratification through confessional tales, but rather a "significant part of the mechanisms of normalisation that clients use to understand their behaviour not as 'deviant' but as acceptable",[64] then the female authored memoir can be similarly positioned as a consciousness-raising exercise. Understood in this way, erotic memoirs serve to publicise and normalise female promiscuity in a world where female sexuality is sub-ject to constraints, control and condemnation. Just as the Internet has provided an anonymous space for male clients of sex workers to lay bare their intimate selves, the memoir has provided a similar space for female writers to present permanent and public testimonies of their engagement in the sexual world and abilities to perform as sexual beings.

The anonymous spaces of the virtual and the memoir provide a lib-erating context to women who normally feel disenfranchised in their everyday communities and who can convene and become normative. In

DOI: 10.1057/9781137326546

the context of male sexuality, this manifests itself through sites such as *PunterNet*, where men can locate and communicate with each other as a homogenous yet stigmatised social group: clients of sex workers. In the context of female sexuality, blogs such as Abby Lee's *Girl With a One Track Mind* function to publicise narratives of female desire as a form of consciousness-raising exercise, allowing the possibility of dialogue with women who share her perspective on the moral economy of sex. Virtual meeting spaces overcome physical barriers and societal judgements that produce shame and embarrassment, allowing individuals to gain support in a non-stigmatising environment. From this coming together of identities, women may gain freedom from the constraints placed on their sexual expression and identity by everyday expectations of sexual decorum. The Internet has served to make this process incredibly simple, and in theorising the compatibility of sexuality and cyberspace, Cooper *et al.*[65] have defined the "Triple-A-Engine" that makes "the virtual" so attractive for sexual pursuits. These attractions of accessibility, affordability and anonymity have primarily been understood in contemporary sexological research as motivating factors that encourage men to employ online facilities to explore the commercial sex industry. Sanders comments that, "There are no longer real-time constraints that limit opportunities to explore different markets, meet sex workers and make informed choices about who to visit and what service to buy",[66] and contemporary women's memoirs exploit these virtual opportunities in seeking out hookup sex. Women's memoirs not only document the convenience of employing the Internet to find sex but, perhaps more interestingly, document the dramatic role that technology occupies in the growth and decline of intimate relationships.

In Townsend's *Sleeping Around: Secrets of a Sexual Adventuress*, the author identifies this as a peculiarly British trend: "In the States the text is considered a mere rest stop on the superhighway of love – a check-in point between phone calls. But in the UK some of my friends have had entire relationships that started, bloomed and were finally extinguished via a two-inch screen."[67] And yet, many popular memoirs reveal the growth of emotional intimacy through virtual communication to be a global trend. Tracy Quan's *Diary of a Married Call Girl* (2006) presents an interaction between the semi-fictional narrator, Nancy Chan, and her best friend Allie, and the latter – preparing for a first face-to-face meeting with a man after several Internet conversations – asks "don't you think this is more like a *third* date? Or even a fifth?". Allie's sense

DOI: 10.1057/9781137326546

of heightened intimacy – despite having never met the man – is based on the fact that they spent "two hours IM-ing about the problems in his mother's homeland" and exchanged "articulate" and "sensitive"[68] emails. Dawn Porter's memoir registers a similar social trend through a sardonic evaluation of her lover's former relationship: "It was a woman that he met through an American site. They got talking, they had a lot in common; he liked the sound of her, she liked the sound of him. They talked for months, exchanged pictures, had phone conversations and fell in love with each other as much as you possibly can when you haven't even smelled, met or touched each other."[69]

Despite Porter's cynicism, her own memoir corroborates the impact of the Internet on the growth of emotional intimacy. Her memoir confirms not only the convenience of making initial contact through dating websites, but also a sense of psychological closeness fostered by email interaction: "When I Internet dated there was a genuine connection from the initial email contact. This connection could be anything from a common interest to a similar sense of humour, or even an unspoken sexual attraction that managed to seep its way through the words."[70] Even though Porter has to sift through "pictures of cocks" and "descriptions of sexual abilities" before achieving some form of emotional exchange, she manages to "get some email banter going with some people who interested [her] enough to want to meet them".[71] After meeting these virtual conquests in the real world, Porter finds that online preliminaries ensure that first-date conversations "flowed well as we already knew so much about each other".[72]

Krissy Kneen's *Affection* positions the Internet as an extraordinarily powerful tool in transforming the erotic imagination. After meeting a potential lover, Paul, on only one occasion, she begins to meet him online for several consecutive evenings until realising that "This Paul is now someone I know from the Internet more than real life", and confesses: "I don't even remember what Paul looks likes, just a vague impression, but we talk every night. I feel like his voice is my own voice, and I feel an attraction built on disembodied words."[73] Kneen proceeds to reveal how this attraction, "built on disembodied words", can lead to addictive behaviours that parallel the consumption of alternative forms of online entertainment: "I look out for him, switching between Internet pornography and Facebook, where I will be able to see if he has come online. I am disappointed that he does not. I chat with someone else briefly, and without the same kind of connection. I find that I miss him; that I was

DOI: 10.1057/9781137326546

looking forward to another conversation."[74] What remains clear over the course of several memoirs is that while the emotional and sexual relationships developed through cyberspace serve to explain, at least partially, the popularity of Internet dating, a plethora of other factors are at play.

Indeed, Porter comments that, "On the site I was anonymous, so no one knew anything about me. It was up to me how much information I divulged as there was no profile form to fill in, unlike many dating sites."[75] For Porter, the appeal of virtual dating lies in the anonymity it provides, which she positions as essential when performing sexual identities that transgress conventional femininity, hence the need to establish contact with "total randoms in a totally disconnected way from every day stuff".[76] What Porter is perhaps trying to convey, albeit not very eloquently, is that it is only through anonymous encounters ("total randoms") and only through anonymity ("totally disconnected way from every day stuff") that female sexuality can be fully explored, not least because demonstrations of overt female desire often lead women, in real life scenarios, into encounters where male force is exerted: "And if at any time the banter made me feel threatened or uncomfortable, I could pull out instantly."[77] The Internet also provides an outlet for the performance of multiple feminine identities, some neo-traditional, others distinctly postfeminist: "What's fascinated me most out of all this is how I react differently to different people. With some people I may be the consummate lady, with others I'm a brazen hussy who can't wait to get my pants off; yet I'm always myself."[78] Abby Lee expresses a similar sentiment in confessing to being "intrigued by the way people take on different identities online", ensuring that it is "easier by far to chat someone up".[79] What both Porter and Lee demonstrate is that the construction of a "new" or plural identity, either anonymous or performed allows women to negotiate the prescriptions of conventional femininity where female sexual conduct is strictly regulated. And it is precisely due to the liberating possibilities of cyberspace that many popular women's memoirs engage in a process of destigmatising online exchanges.

Porter's memoir recounts a meeting with a man who "spoke very openly about the fact that he saw no shame in meeting people on the Net",[80] while Townsend rationalises that "clicking on a profile is no more random than bumping into someone in a bar" and therefore finds it "strange that people are still embarrassed to admit they met online".[81] Yet, in contrast to Porter, Townsend is typically perceptive and, while

DOI: 10.1057/9781137326546

recognising the convenience of Internet dating ("I can flirt in my slippers"), also acknowledges its limitations through observations that are far more nuanced:

> But I soon remembered why I had tired of Internet dating in the first place: the profiles all seemed to merge into one. I enjoy candlelit dinners as much as the next girl, but I'm perplexed by guys like "Ready4therealthing" who list "long walks on the beach" and "soulful conversation" as interests. It's as if men have compiled a list of what they think women want, drawing inspiration only from the covers of romance novels.[82]

Thus while the memoirs discussed so far demonstrate that even though the Internet may offer limitless opportunities for both hookup sex and the development of emotional intimacy, it is necessary to question the extent to which the interplay between "authenticity" and "performance" complicates burgeoning sexual and emotional relationships. An exploration of the role of authenticity in intimate exchanges is perhaps most achievable by examining the manner in which popular women's memoirs collapse the space between authentic/non-commercial and performative/commercial sexual exchanges.

Intimacy and commercial sex

The rise of the Internet as a place of intimate exchange marks the breakdown of global patterns whereby intimacy is historically forged on sustained contact between two parties and the commensurate blossoming of emotional and physical relationships. Popular women's memoirs demonstrate that, in accordance with Giddens' view of "plastic sexuality" – terms of sexual exchange freed from their intrinsic relation to reproduction – traditional and historical understanding of the ostensibly inseparable connection between sex and intimacy must now be read as highly problematic and far too inflexible. Perhaps nowhere are the complexities of intimacy more apparent than in the memoirs' construction of commercial sexual exchange, serving to rebuke perceptions of the client–sex worker relationship as one marked by clear and indissoluble roles, boundaries and functions. In many ways, women's memoirs attest to the diversity and plurality of commercial sexual relationships, and more importantly, collapse the emotional space between commercial and non-commercial sex. It is in this way that erotic memoirs corroborate

DOI: 10.1057/9781137326546

sociological research on sex work which navigates the convoluted territory of intimacy in sexual transactions.

Teela Sanders defines the client–sex worker exchange as dominated by three common patterns, arguing that while genuine mutuality in emotional and sexual exchange certainly exists, experiences of mutual emotional and physical satisfaction are complicated by "delusions of mutuality". Sanders defines genuine mutuality as an exchange in which authentic "mutual pleasure is experienced by both parties either inside or outside the professional boundaries of commercial sex", a form of intimacy that is widely experienced but often obscured by the "authentic" delusion of mutuality and the "authentic–fake" delusion of mutuality. She proceeds to define the former as "Acting (i.e. not pleasure) by the sex worker is necessary to provide the illusion of mutual pleasure yet is experienced by the client as genuine mutual pleasure" and the latter as where the "client understands that the sex worker is acting as part of the service" yet still "experiences the interaction as mutual and authentic even though both parties are aware it is fake".[83] The visible complexity of the emotional and sexual dynamics at play contravenes the widely held perception of commercial sex as nothing more than a transactional experience, which functions as a necessary component of the separation of emotions, intimacy and sex.

The classic feminist critique of sex work as a form of exploitation and commodification of women's bodies has, ironically, ensured that – for the male client at least – the experience of commercial sexual transaction remains morally unproblematic. Anti-prostitution scholars like Sheila Jeffreys dehumanise "the prostituted woman"[84] and see her as someone who lacks agency and subjectivity, which arguably makes it infinitely easier for men to abdicate responsibility from the wider issues of exploitation and ethics. Yet, there are two accounts on which this simplification of what occurs in the sex industry can be challenged. First, the argument of objectification ignores that there are, as widely documented, emotional aspects to the client–sex worker relationship, and second, it ignores that many clients place a low priority on sex and a higher priority on emotional connection. Certainly, even though the subjective experience of intimacy is impossible to measure with any degree of specificity, it is the lived experience of perceived intimacy that complicates traditional configurations of sex work as a purely physical experience. Teela Sanders has observed that "the desire for emotional intimacy as well as physical intimacy leads men to become regulars to the same sex worker and

DOI: 10.1057/9781137326546

develop a relationship that mirrors heterosexual male romantic scripts"[85] involving, but not limited to, an overnight stay, dinner, dancing, kissing in public and being considered a "couple".

This perhaps explains why, in Jenny Angell's *Callgirl*, the narrator stresses that her "agency had clients who wanted education, clients who presumably wanted to talk intelligently with their escorts, who were looking for something beyond firm breasts and empty thoughts".[86] The higher the educational and social skills of the escort, the easier it is for the client–sex worker relationship to follow the rituals of courtship, which may or may not comprise bringing gifts, promoting the feelings and pleasures of companionship and romance. In Abby Lee's *Girl With a One Track Mind*, the author describes the "Girlfriend Experience" of sex work, stating that in these encounters clients "get sex, a cuddle and a chance to offload what's on their mind", a space in which men can "maintain the charade that all they want is a shag"[87] by paying for the experience. In Lee's understanding, the sex worker–client relationship allows men to shore up their masculinity while satisfying a desire for emotional companionship. In this instance, the distance between commercial and non-commercial sex can be collapsed, and the performance of hegemonic masculinity grounded in sexual expression masks a more authentic desire for emotional fulfilment.

Tracy Quan's *Diary of a Manhattan Call Girl* (2001) demonstrates a similar dissolution of the boundaries between performed and authentic sexual scripts. In Quan's account of commercial exchanges, the vocalisation of authentic pleasure exists in a taboo territory all of its own, often contravening the sexual codes and social etiquette of the sex worker–client relationship by colonising the commercial sexual encounter with feelings of sexual desire that one would expect to experience only in a non-commercial encounter. Quan depicts, in a contradictory manner that exposes the complexity of the sexual exchange, authentic physical pleasure as a performed service for the client, commenting that she "felt obliged to throw in a real orgasm" as "A man won't think of you as a pleasure-pinching hooker if you take a little time out for an orgasm".[88] In this account, authenticity and performativity are interdependent, suggesting that any attempt to locate the commercial encounter as polarised by either "genuine" or "fake" experiences is extremely problematic. What many memoirs reveal, then, is the attempts by both sex workers and clients to negotiate the prescriptive social conventions of sex work.

DOI: 10.1057/9781137326546

During one encounter in Quan's sequel, *Diary of a Married Call Girl* (2005), in which her narrator Nancy Chan has a MFF threesome, she acknowledges the performativity of "Jasmine's fake sound effects", yet also confesses to her own socially inappropriate but entirely authentic sexual desire: "As I touched myself, I kept hoping she wouldn't suspect me of enjoying her tongue. I wondered if I might even get away with coming, but Jasmine was just too near. She would be horrified if she figured it out!"[89] There remains, in many of Quan's accounts of sex work, the recognition that sexual authenticity is a personal and intimate expression of selfhood that somehow upsets the dynamics of commercial sex: "I opened my legs wider and gave him what I'd been waiting for, as quietly as I could. When I came, I felt my stomach contracting – because I was trying not to make the telltale sounds. Yes, he did seduce me. Successfully. But I still don't want Roland to know what I'm 'really' like. It's a sneaky, surreptitious climax – not a wild noisy release. Noise is reserved for those times when I'm faking it."[90]

Chan's memoir publicises her sexual pleasure, but only retrospectively after the encounter is over, suggesting that while commercial sex is often a site of emotional and physical exchange not dissimilar from non-commercial sex, overt expressions of sexual pleasure and intimacy in commercial encounters place deviant and normative sexuality in close proximity. Yet, it is important to recognise that one of the reasons why so many memoirs collapse the space between "performative" and "authentic" sexuality is because the experience of being a sex worker is positioned as so similar to the experience of being a woman in a heterosexual, non-commercial sexual relationship. In Portnoy's *The Butcher, the Baker, the Candlestick Maker* (2006), the narrator soon realises that she is "one small step away from becoming a professional" after numerous encounters in which her mind is "disconnected from the action". In a confession that reveals the impact of both the mainstreaming of the sex industry and the ubiquity of cyberporn, Portnoy comments that whether with "Greg or Oliver or Tim or Anthony or Dave or whoever", all sexual encounters are ultimately mediated by the "porn fantasy in [her] head, usually one that did not involve the person [she] was actually with".[91]

Portnoy's confession raises important questions regarding contemporary women's inability to negotiate pleasurable sexual experiences, and serves to dispel the notion that prostitutes and non-prostitutes always experience sex in polarised ways. In a similar manner, Jenny Angell's

Callgirl testifies to the fact that many commercial sexual encounters can be as romantic and sexually tentative as those experienced at the beginning of heterosexual love relationships: "We sat on a small sofa in the cabin of his sailboat, drank a very nice chilled Montrachet, and talked about music, our conversation interspersed with clumsy silences. It felt oddly familiar, as if ... well, to tell you the truth, what it felt like was a date. A first date. A blind date."[92] In this encounter, the client asks the narrator if he may put his arm around her body, and the narrator perceives the advance to be "endearing beyond belief".[93] Angell's narrator recognises the industry conventions and constraints of sex work, commenting that "some callgirls won't kiss" as they "consider their lips the only part of themselves that they can withhold", yet refuses to follow the same pattern, arguing that in the absence of real intimacy "the pretence of romance is better than no romance at all".[94] Once again, we see the performative and the authentic dissolved, suggesting that even though popular conceptions of authentic intimacy place it firmly in specific contexts, namely monogamous and romantic love relationships, intimacy as a performed social convention can occur in a number of contexts.

This chapter has sought to explore the negotiation of sexual and emotional intimacy in a number of ways. In examining how popular women's memoirs construct intimacy in the 21st century, it is clear that some of these memoirs identify emotional intimacy as an unplanned consequence of sexual pleasure, while others remain trapped in romantic ideologies that construct sex and love as interdependent. The latter position sexual encounters as a necessary compromise on the journey to emotional intimacy, a form of currency that can ensure the successful purchase of love. We have witnessed how sex functions to expunge a variety of negative experiences and memories, especially those experiences involving pain and vulnerability, and even how sex functions as a site for rearticulating childhood trauma. Even though all of the memoirs position some form of emotional investment as central to sexual encounters, we have also witnessed how many memoirs position sexual exchanges as characterised by a movement between an absence of emotional intimacy and an abundance of emotional intimacy. In fact, many memoirs depict good sex as an outcome of conflicting feelings of love and hate, a transaction where lovers are not emotionally distant but where emotional proximity is saturated with the memories of negative, as much as positive, shared experiences.

This chapter has also explored the impact of the growth of the Internet on intimacy and sexual behaviour, documented in memoirs that position

DOI: 10.1057/9781137326546

cyberspace as a facilitating mechanism for "hookup sex". We have witnessed how women's memoirs corroborate the impact of the Internet in transforming their understanding of emotional intimacy, not merely in the convenience of making initial contact through dating websites, but also through a sense of psychological closeness fostered by email and online interaction. Yet perhaps most importantly, for many contemporary women, the appeal of virtual dating surely lies in the anonymity it provides, which the memoirs position as essential when performing a sexual identity that transgresses conventional femininity. In many ways, then, the intimate genre of the memoir opens up a space for women to negotiate the types of intimacy that society deems acceptable and gender appropriate, and in doing so reveals the instability and fallacies of such constructions.

Notes

1   Robert Jensen, *Getting Off: Pornography and the End of Masculinity* (Cambridge, MA: South End Press, 2007), 154.

2   Naomi Wolf, *Promiscuities: A Secret History of Female Desire* (London: Vintage, 1998), 114.

3   Lynne Jamieson, *Intimacies: Personal Relationships in Modern Societies* (Cambridge: Polity Press, 1988), 133.

4   Ibid., 134.

5   Natasha Walter, *Living Dolls: The Return of Sexism* (London: Virago, 2010), 101.

6   Jeffrey Weeks, *Sexuality* (London and New York: Routledge, 2003), 114.

7   Anthony Giddens, *The Transformation of Intimacy: Sexuality, Love and Eroticism in Modern Societies* (Cambridge: Polity Press, 1992), 45–66.

8   Jamieson, *Intimacies*, 109.

9   Teela Sanders, *Paying for Pleasure: Men Who Buy Sex* (Portland, OR: Willan Publishing, 2008), 88.

10   Weeks, *Sexuality*, 1.

11   Shere Hite, *The Hite Report on the Family: Growing Up under Patriarchy* (London: Bloomsbury, 1994), 73.

12   Jamieson, *Intimacies*, 133.

13   Harry Brod, "Pornography and the Alienation of Male Sexuality" in *Sexual Lives: A Reader on the Theories and Realities of Human Sexuality*, eds Betsy Crane and Robert Heasley (New York: McGraw-Hill, 2003), 478.

14   Jamieson, *Intimacies*, 106.

15   Toni Bentley, *The Surrender: An Erotic Memoir* (London: Harper Perennial, 2006), 162.

DOI: 10.1057/9781137326546

16   Ibid., 133.
17   Melissa P., *One Hundred Strokes of the Brush before Bed*, trans. Lawrence Venuti (London: Serpent's Tail, 2004), 109.
18   Ibid., 14.
19   Ibid., 118.
20   Abby Lee, *Girl with a One Track Mind: Confessions of the Seductress Next Door* (London: Ebury Press, 2006), 40.
21   Ibid., 150.
22   Catherine Millet, *The Sexual Life of Catherine M.*, trans. Adriana Hunter (London: Corgi Books, 2003 [2002]), 22.
23   Ibid., 79.
24   Melissa P., *One Hundred Strokes*, 72.
25   Ibid., 19.
26   Bentley, *The Surrender*, 159.
27   Ibid., 135.
28   Ibid., 30.
29   Catherine Townsend, *Breaking the Rules: Confessions of a Bad Girl* (London: John Murray, 2008), 21–22.
30   Lee, *Girl with a One Track Mind*, 118.
31   Bentley, *The Surrender*, 10.
32   Ibid., 105.
33   Townsend, *Breaking the Rules*, 164.
34   Ibid., 171.
35   Lynne Segal, *Is the Future Female?: Trouble Thoughts on Contemporary Feminism* (London: Virago, 1987), 72.
36   Krissy Kneen, *Affection: An Erotic Memoir* (Berkeley, California: Seal Press, 2010), 158.
37   Kathrina Glitre, "Nancy Meyers and Popular Feminism" in *Women on Screen: Feminism and Femininity in Visual Culture*, ed. Melanie Waters (Basingstoke: Palgrave Macmillan, 2011), 28.
38   Gail Dines, *Pornland: How Porn Has Hijacked Our Sexuality* (Boston, MA: Beacon Press, 2010), 63.
39   Walter, *Living Dolls*, 109.
40   Ibid., 95.
41   Jensen, *Getting Off*, 159.
42   Kneen, *Affection*, 55.
43   Dines, *Pornland*, 114.
44   Ibid.
45   Dawn Porter, *Diaries of an Internet Lover* (London: Virgin Books, 2006), 1.
46   Ibid.
47   Ibid., 103.

DOI: 10.1057/9781137326546

48 Belle de Jour , *The Intimate Adventures of a London Call Girl* (London: Phoenix, 2005), 177.

49 Jenny Angell, *Callgirl* (London: Avon, 2007), 89.

50 Almudena Grandes, *The Ages of Lulu*, trans. Sonia Soto (London: Phoenix, 2005 [1993]), 46.

51 Catherine Townsend, *Sleeping Around: Secrets of a Sexual Adventuress* (London: John Murray, 2007), 124–125.

52 Bentley, *The Surrender*, 106.

53 Ibid., 52.

54 Townsend, *Breaking the Rules*, 25.

55 Ibid., 184.

56 Suzanne Portnoy, *The Butcher, the Baker, the Candlestick Maker* (London: Virgin Books, 2006), 144.

57 Lee, *Girl with a One Track Mind*, 102.

58 Ibid., 99.

59 Angell, *Callgirl*, 47.

60 Portnoy, *The Butcher*, 46.

61 Sanders, *Paying for Pleasure*, 62.

62 Ibid., 67.

63 Ibid.

64 Ibid., 69.

65 Al Cooper et al., "Sexuality in Cyberspace: Update for the 21st Century", *CyberPsychology and Behaviour* 3, vol. 4 (2000): 522.

66 Sanders, *Paying for Pleasure*, 70.

67 Townsend, *Sleeping Around*, 197.

68 Tracy Quan, *Diary of a Married Call Girl* (London: Harper Perennial, 2006 [2005]), 4.

69 Porter, *Diaries of an Internet Lover*, 141.

70 Ibid., 3.

71 Ibid., 5.

72 Ibid., 3.

73 Ibid., 57.

74 Ibid., 33.

75 Porter, *Diaries of an Internet Lover*, 5.

76 Ibid., 19.

77 Ibid., 5.

78 Ibid., 4.

79 Ibid., 85.

80 Ibid., 38.

81 Townsend, *Breaking the Rules*, 158.

82 Ibid.

DOI: 10.1057/9781137326546

83   Sanders, *Paying for Pleasure*, 99.
84   Sheila Jeffreys, *The Industrial Vagina: The Political Economy of the Global Sex Trade.* (London and New York: Routledge, 2009), 17.
85   Ibid., 91.
86   Angell, *Callgirl*, 35.
87   Lee, *Girl with a One Track Mind*, 107.
88   Tracy Quan, *Diary of a Manhattan Call Girl* (London: Harper Perennial, 2005 [2001]), 41.
89   Quan, *Diary of a Married Call Girl*, 41.
90   Ibid., 98.
91   Portnoy, *The Butcher*, 156.
92   Angell, *Callgirl*, 19.
93   Ibid., 20.
94   Ibid., 22.

DOI: 10.1057/9781137326546

3
Pornography

Abstract: *This chapter explores the impact of pornography on contemporary culture and attempts to position women's erotic memoirs in the nebulous space between "pornography" and "erotica". It argues that while women's erotic memoirs are inherently concordant with erotica, postfeminist culture and the mainstreaming of pornography have coopted and colonised the genre. The chapter suggests that the memoirs under discussion inhabit a space that is both progressive and regressive – a challenge to and an affirmation of conventional femininity – the former by forcefully expressing a postfeminist female agency in their (visual) consumption of male and female bodies, and the latter by adhering to the ideological and aesthetic conventions of male-produced pornography.*

Gwynne, Joel. *Erotic Memoirs and Postfeminism: The Politics of Pleasure.* Basingstoke: Palgrave Macmillan, 2013.
DOI: 10.1057/9781137326546.

The history of pornography has largely concerned the written word, yet the genre remains predominantly understood in terms of both visual culture and mass consumption. In contrast, erotic literature, or "erotica", is usually understood to be non-visual and produced for a comparatively narrow audience. In visual culture, pornography remains essentially unconcerned with character development and human motivation as representing the details of sexual acts and bodily sensations are of primary importance.[1] To locate contemporary women's erotic memoirs in debates concerning the definition of pornography and erotica entails the negotiation of a number of divisive, intersecting and nebulous territories. It is, in fact, often highly difficult to position women's memoirs when attempting to understand them as works of either "pornography" or "erotica", primarily due to the fact that neither of these terms – nor their corresponding associations – are entirely appropriate in describing the form and function of the non-fiction genre. Erotica is usually defined as a fictionalised literary genre understood "as a realm of fantasy, play, and experimentation" and is "linked to aesthetic notions of quality",[2] while the definition of pornography rests on detailed yet hyperbolic depictions of sexual arousal, scenarios, acts, and sensations with the purpose of eliciting arousal in the audience. The affective power of pornography depends on the authenticity of these explicit representations, while the affective power of erotica revolves around the characters' articulation of sexual desire and their emotional and psychological investment in sexual encounters. Such aesthetic divergences are further complicated by Dana Wilson-Kovacs' comment that "Erotica is associated with women while porn is associated with men",[3] marking pornography and erotica as distinctly gendered spaces. Pornographic formulas are often perceived by women as, if not offensive, limited in scope, full of reductive meanings and predictable action, while erotica is seen as catering to women in a more "approachable" and "understanding" manner. As Clarissa Smith astutely notes, despite the fact that pornography is occasionally produced for a female audience, there remains widespread theorisations of pornography "as a field of representation and consumption inimitable to women's experiences of sexuality".[4]

For this reason, sexually explicit memoirs written by women are by default positioned as inherently concordant with erotica – a genre that is textual rather than visual, primarily female-authored rather than male-produced – and when approaching the genre readers could be forgiven for not only expecting a certain attention to both characterisation and

DOI: 10.1057/9781137326546

the description of tactile sensations, but also writing that is of a high literary quality for precisely these reasons. However, despite this expectation, the majority of the memoirs discussed in this book are, like visual pornography, produced for mass consumption and are non-literary, therefore complicating not only existing gendered definitions of erotica and pornography but also their corresponding notions of aesthetic quality. The memoirs convene elements of both erotica and pornography and what could perhaps be identified, somewhat traditionally, as "male" and "female" textual subjectivities. In feminist terms, the ramifications of this integration are especially problematic, for erotica has been historically embraced by feminist scholars while pornography has been largely contested, raising a critical question: How should we position female-authored memoirs that appear to embrace the aesthetic notions and ideological assumptions of male-produced visual pornography? This question becomes particularly complex when we acknowledge that the form of the memoir has been historically positioned as inherently feminist, and has been especially important in the ascent of third-wave feminism.

In *Promiscuities: A Secret History of Female Desire* (1998), Naomi Wolf attests to the role of memoirs in feminist consciousness-raising, commenting that "there is something missing from our psychological understanding of how girls become women today that only first-person accounts can fill".[5] Similarly, Jennifer Baumgardner and Amy Richards observe that in historical terms, "women's personal stories have been the evidence of where the movement needs to go politically".[6] Given the regulation of female sexuality and the taboo of female promiscuity, the act of writing a sexual history embodies potential implications that are especially damaging to women, constituting a "record that can be used to embarrass, belittle or even destroy".[7] For this reason, the decision to make public a private sexual history can be positioned as a subversive political act in itself, and this political intent has been evident in the form of feminist memoirs such as Elizabeth Wurtzel's *Prozac Nation* (1994) and Leora Tanenbaum's *Slut! Growing Up Female with a Bad Reputation* (1999). Yet, despite what the feminist imperatives that the mere act of producing a public sexual history may signify, the memoirs discussed in this book make no obvious claim to a conspicuous feminist politics, and their nebulous position between erotica and pornography further complicates the potential liberatory sensibilities that the texts may espouse. Prior to exploring this further, it is imperative to contextualise recent debates surrounding pornography and their feminist interventions.

DOI: 10.1057/9781137326546

Censorship, anti-censorship and popular culture

Even though second-wave feminist debates on pornography began more than 30 years ago, the vestiges of these debates still rage today. In the 21st century, Feona Attwood invokes the spectre of the pro and anti-censorship campaigns of the 1980s in her nuanced observation that contemporary online pornographies resurrect earlier configurations of pornography as "framed in two quite distinct ways", as either "a brave new frontier for sexual expression" or a "perilous vortex of danger and corruption".[8] Erotic memoirs summon debates surrounding new forms of pornography, which include not only the growth of Internet pornography but also print pornography and erotica. They also serve to rearticulate concerns about the alleged negative effects of pornography on beliefs, attitudes, and behaviour, especially "the encouragement of violence against women, the endorsement of sexist and misogynist views, the destruction of childhood innocence, and the commodification of relationships".[9] Jeffrey Weeks summarises the real-world implications of these concerns by commenting that feminist protest against pornography and sadomasochistic practices "relies on the argument that representations of violence can cause violence", and that "sexual behaviour which flirts with power imbalances can sustain existing power relations".[10]

Indeed, even though there is "no litmus test [for] what is or is not pornography",[11] the pioneering work of pro-censorship feminist activism successfully identified a number of characteristics unique to heterosexual pornography such as the positioning of women as naturally subordinate to men; the eroticisation of men's social and physical power over women; the depiction of aggression – both sexual and non-sexual – as the inevitable result of such power imbalances; and the undermining of social barriers and conventions by the apparently relentless power of sex.[12] Lynne Segal summarises the pro-censorship position on pornography thus: "as well as teaching women their place as whores, pornography also serves as ubiquitous propaganda, spurring on the flagging or wimpish male to ever greater acts of violence against women".[13] Yet, this position, despite being the dominant perspective associated with second-wave radical feminist responses to the sex industry, has been disputed by a vocal minority: "The excuse for banning 'violent' porn is that this will end violence against women. The causal connection is dubious. It is indisputably true that very few people who consume pornography ever assault or rape another person."[14] It is in this minefield of political dissent that we

DOI: 10.1057/9781137326546

approach erotic women's writing, the discussion and evaluation of which is more pertinent in the 21st century than ever before, for many women who would describe themselves as feminists have "come to accept that they are growing up in a world where pornography is ubiquitous and will be part of almost everyone's sexual experiences".[15]

Contrary to this pragmatic response, contemporary acceptance of pornography is often politically motivated. Linda Williams argues that feminists like herself have come to recognise that pro-censorship campaigns serve to "emphasize woman's role as the absolute victim of male sadism" and "perpetuate the supposedly essential nature of woman's powerlessness".[16] Debates that attempt to position pornography as not necessarily damaging to women, and perhaps even liberating, have emerged in force in the late-20th century, arguably because the consumption of pornography by women has become a marked feature of popular culture in the 21st century. Pornography has become mainstream, in accordance with a neo-liberal embracement of the potentially empowering possibilities offered to women by the sex industry, heralding a new trajectory of sexual representation in popular culture. In *Pornland: How Porn Has Hijacked Our Sexuality* (2010), anti-porn scholar Gail Dines declares that "in the past, porn performers couldn't shake the sleaze factor and were hence considered untouchable by most mainstream pop culture industries."[17] Dines laments the positive media reception to Jenna Jameson's career as a testimony to the popularisation of the sex industry, commenting that the former porn star "managed to break through the porn barrier by moving seamlessly between the porn world and mainstream media".[18] Jameson has undeniably emerged as a dominant figure in American popular culture, as not only a former porn star but also as an entrepreneur and celebrity, featuring as a regular attraction in lifestyle magazines such as *People* and *Us Weekly*, on television channels such as VH1, E! Entertainment and HBO, and in advertisements for Abercrombie & Fitch. Like a host of transatlantic cultural commentators, including the popular journalists Ariel Levy and Natasha Walter, Dines has identified Jameson's crossover success from porn idol to popular icon as emblematic of contemporary permissiveness surrounding the sex industry (pornography, prostitution and stripping), commenting that "the hypersexualization of mass-produced images" has "crowded out any alternative images of being female".[19]

The wider culture supports this view. Magazine content in mainstream men's, women's and teen magazines is increasingly sexually

DOI: 10.1057/9781137326546

explicit with covers routinely mentioning orgasm and sexual techniques, while a recent study of magazines targeting teen girls found "an average of more than 80 column inches of text per issue on sexual topics".[20] Katherine Kinnick suggests that while teen girls have always engaged in boy-chasing, "porn culture has ratcheted up what girls feel they must do to win the guy: from dressing and dancing in an overly provocative manner to engaging in sexual behaviors that are staples of male porn."[21] While this may appear to be harmless performance, Mardia Bishop highlights the potential negative effects on women's negotiation of sexual boundaries and sexual decision-making: "Girls are learning that sex is one-sided, that it is something they are to provide for the pleasure of boys."[22] In accordance, debates have emerged surrounding not only children's access to sexual content in media, and the effects of media consumption on their sexual knowledge, attitudes and behaviours, but also the detrimental effects of porn culture on adults. Plastic surgeons in the US are experiencing an explosion in the demand for breast implants and vaginoplasty, while the consumption of erotic products is frequently presented as the most effective means by which a woman can signal her status as a liberated, independent woman.

Critical discussion of pornography has been further complicated since the ascent of postfeminism as a cultural condition, and in *Living Dolls: The Return of Sexism* (2010), Natasha Walter comments that second-wave feminist critiques of pornography shared a common misconception: "they assumed that women never take any pleasure in pornography".[23] Yet, while a plethora of evidence supports Walter's claim – not least the popularity and growth of UK retailers like Ann Summers who sell sex toys in addition to lingerie – the extent to which women take pleasure in pornography, and the extent to which women are coerced into consuming pornography, is somewhat difficult to determine due to the cultural impositions and social pressures presented within postfeminist cultural praxis. Charting the growth of "raunch culture" and "do-me-feminism", Genz and Brabon highlight that women are now encouraged to express individual agency "not by politicising [their] relationships with men and [their] status as a sexual object but primarily through the re-articulation of [their] feminine/sexual identity".[24] Commenting on the recuperation of the girl as an empowering figure in postfeminist culture, Imelda Whelehan states that this reconfiguration "only notionally offers a subversion of the pin-up image: she is active rather than passive, and ruthlessly self-seeking in her own pleasures. Outspoken and sometimes

DOI: 10.1057/9781137326546

aggressive, the new girl has no truck with feminine wiles, yet she looks deceptively like a pin-up."[25] The recuperation of the girl as a sexually active rather than sexually subordinate figure demonstrates the prevalence of a vision of women's empowerment that is deeply complicit in porn culture. Popular women's memoirs corroborate this inability for female self-definition outside of porn, and in Catherine Townsend's *Sleeping Around: Secrets of a Sexual Adventuress* (2007), the narrator comments: "Given that pornography has become so ubiquitous in popular culture, I'm often surprised that boys seem shocked when I mention my personal porn collection."[26] What this reveals is not only an awareness that pornography has saturated the public space of popular culture, but also the personal impact in the private space.

This chapter seeks to explore women's erotic memoirs as sites of pornography production, with the aim of answering the following questions: In what way do these memoirs demonstrate how the popularisation of pornography has affected women's sexual lives? More specifically, how do the memoirs' depictions of sexual practices reflect the aesthetic paradigm of pornography, and to what extent does this complicate arguments surrounding the presentation of the female body as agentic?

The pornography paradigm

Commenting on the rise of depilation and cosmetic surgery as one of the many self-regulatory practices performed by contemporary women, Natasha Walter states that the "idea that there is one correct way for female genitals to look is undoubtedly tied into the rise of pornography".[27] In Toni Bentley's *The Surrender: An Erotic Memoir* (2006), the narrator similarly demarcates depilation as a contemporary lifestyle trend that has risen commensurately with the mainstreaming of the sex industry: "I began with the simple side trims, the tutu trim, from my ballet-dancing days – a nice isosceles triangle. But then I went to a few strip clubs and got jealous of those very exposed, hairless pussies."[28] While it is always problematic and potentially disempowering to position any aspect of women's bodily decision-making as socially induced rather than self-individuating, it cannot be denied that Bentley's motivation to remove her pubic hair is not self-determined: the author depilates so her lover can "get a view" and "get access".[29] This confession, and the idolisation of the bodies of strippers, implicitly centralises the growing

DOI: 10.1057/9781137326546

inclination to render sexual encounters as principally visual rather than tactile experiences, in accordance with the values of the sex industry and the accentuation of performance aesthetics. Yet, it is important to note that even though recent women's memoirs all appear to share an equal recognition of the dominance of depilatory practices in contemporary lifestyle culture, they also showcase a number of divergent attitudes to the practice. Depilation is both embraced and critiqued, seen as, on the one hand, a marker of feminine sophistication and, on the other, an unhealthy outcome of the popularisation of the sex industry.

In Tracy Quan's *Diary of a Married Call Girl* (2005), the narrator decrees that the period "before pubic hair got Brazilianized" was "like being preliterate",[30] implying a regressive stage of civilisation and sexual etiquette. She continues to comment that "a hairless pussy is classic" while a "permanent landing strip would date [her]",[31] firmly situating depilation as a fashion aesthetic that holds a specific cultural currency within the contemporary moment. Quan's position is apolitical, and Stephanie Genz and Benjamin Brabon argue that the cultural pervasion of postfeminist rhetoric can be attributed to its refusal to challenge patriarchy, its "individualising and commoditising effects that co-opt and undermine feminist content/politics by presenting the production of femininity as entirely self-willed".[32] In the context of Quan's memoir, the narrator's perspective on depilation can be seen as an undermining of feminist politics by refusing to critique or resist its endemic normalisation within culture. In fact, Quan even comments that if a woman allows her pubic hair to grow, this will not "look simple and carefree" but rather "look like you're taking a stand, refusing to wax".[33] For Quan, to resist depilation is akin to self-identification as a radical feminist, an attitude that politically disenfranchises both women who are feminists and choose to depilate, and those who are feminists and choose not to. While the narrator of Sienna Lewis' *Intimate Adventures of an Office Girl* (2009) admits to following the cultural pattern by conceding, "Now I wax my moustache, pluck my eyebrows, shave my legs up to the knees, prune my bikini line, shave it all off", she continues to predict that "we'll all end up lying in a mould of wax once a week, then have it all ripped off so we can be smooth, scentless, androgynous, anorexic porn addicts".[34] Lewis rightly positions depilation as central to contemporary notions of sexual desirability, and the critique inherent in her reference to "anorexic porn addicts" can be located in counterpoint to earlier constructions of sexual desirability: "I remember reading in my parents' *The Joy of Sex* that you

DOI: 10.1057/9781137326546

shouldn't shave your pits because hair traps pheromones and your lover can bury his nose in them and get turned on. That was the seventies. Different story in the noughties."[35]

In the noughties, the transformation of sexual mores can perhaps be attributed not merely to the proliferation of porn chic in popular culture, but more specifically to the addictive behaviour it generates. While Quan comments that a client's "bottomless appetite for porn videos, awkward positions, and oversize sex toys doesn't turn [her] on",[36] women's memoirs chart both male and female addition to pornography. The narrator of Krissy Kneen's *Affection: An Erotic Memoir* (2010) confesses that downloading porn "quick little shots of the stuff, consumed like amyl nitrate",[37] aids her writing process, and Melissa P. logs on and searches for "everything that simultaneously excites and sickens", an "excitement born from humiliation" hoping to meet "the most bizarre individuals, people who send me sadomasochistic photos, who treat [her] like a real whore".[38] And Dawn Porter's memoir suggests that "there are hundreds of women out there with secret desires that they are looking to explore", which includes not merely watching heterosexual male-produced pornography but "horny housewives" producing, exchanging and consuming "naked bath shots, bum shots, tit shots and [...] straight up the middle shots".[39]

Porter's experiences with online pornography parallels a dominant trend in pornography addiction that constructs sexual desire as predicated on the itemisation of male and female anatomy. When visiting a sex museum, Porter is presented with "more images of cocks than [her] poor little clitoris could handle",[40] while Suzanne Portnoy's memoir demonstrates the more detrimental effects of porn addiction. She is only capable of achieving orgasm when she imagines "an entire costume drama in [her] head, complete with a full-scale army in uniform, wounded hero and distraught heroine".[41] What is interesting about Portnoy's confession is not so much the influence of pornography on sexual desire, but the traditionalism of the formulas that precipitate her desire: the active porn hero saving and seducing the passive porn heroine. In fact, despite Catherine Townsend's claim that "female directors such as Candida Royalle and Petra Joy have created an entire genre out of girl-friendly porn",[42] it is remarkable how the porn paradigm in popular women's memoirs does almost nothing to radically restructure the conventions of mass pornography.

These conventions have become increasingly radical in recent years. Speaking of contemporary pornography, Dines states that "images today have now become so extreme that what used to be considered hard-core is now mainstream pornography", and concludes that "acts that are now commonplace in much of online porn were almost nonexistent a couple of decades ago".[43] Similarly, sexual acts performed in mainstream porn have now become normalised in everyday mainstream sexual practices, a pattern that can be partially attributed to sex advice columns in popular journalism. *Cosmopolitan* is a case in point, a magazine that "teaches women how to perform porn sex in a way that is all about male pleasure" and where "technique is the key, and intimacy, love and connection appear only rarely as issues worthy of discussion".[44] Catherine Townsend's *Breaking the Rules: Confessions of a Bad Girl* (2008) can be isolated as a text that particularly highlights the primacy of the porn paradigm in interpersonal relationships. After noticing the effect that women in porn have on her lover – "the girls onscreen were in the 69 position, which only turned him on more" – Townsend responds accordingly: "I wet my hair and lathered up, starting to massage the body wash into my D-cup breasts before soaping further down by sliding my hand between my legs."[45] Performing sexuality in modes of display contingent with pornography becomes the core of Townsend's sexual identity, conspicuous in her description of a MMF threesome: "I could feel the inside walls of my pussy tightening as Mark slammed into me while still massaging my clit, and Russell's rhythmic movements grew more insistent. Then, as my orgasm started to build again, I felt Russell spurt into my mouth."[46]

Her desire to conform to porn practices can perhaps be understood as a desire to establish herself as an empowered woman in a postfeminist climate, where agency is often contingent upon "self-objectification and dependence upon the approving gaze of others".[47] Yet, in order to achieve this "empowerment", Townsend has to acquiesce to a process of self-deindividuation in accordance with pornography's dominant values. In analysing feature and gonzo forms of pornography, Robert Jensen identifies two basic themes common to all mass-marketed heterosexual pornography; the first, that "all women at all times want sex from all men", and the second, that "women like all the sexual acts that men perform or demand".[48] In Jensen's appraisal of pornography, women who do not subscribe to such models of female desire "can be easily turned with a little force", even though "such force is rarely necessary, however, for most of the women in pornography are constructed as the nymphomaniacs men fantasize about".[49] Popular women's memoirs are especially insidious in their complicity in such constructions. Townsend,

DOI: 10.1057/9781137326546

for example, is politically aware, conscious of the historical trajectory of the women's movement, and requests to be treated "like a dirty whore" while acknowledging that "Andrea Dworkin was probably turning in her grave".[50] It is difficult to read this without calling to mind Angela McRobbie's comment that "young women endorse (or else refuse to condemn) the ironic normalization of pornography",[51] for Townsend appears to take great pride in her complicity in the mainstreaming of pornography, demonstrating how "the new female subject is, despite her freedom, called upon to be silent, to withhold critique in order to count as a modern sophisticated girl".[52]

However, at the same time, her desire to simulate pornography practices that centralise male power and female submission needs to be understood in the context of attitudes to sexuality more discursively. Patrick Califia, both a feminist and a sadomasochist practitioner, makes this clear in his incisive observation that, depending on the context, "certain sensations may frighten you, make you angry, urge you on, or get you hot", and that "people choose to endure pain or discomfort if the goal they are striving for makes it worthwhile". By continuing to emphasise that "long-distance runners are not generally thought of as sex perverts, nor is St Theresa", Califia comes to the conclusion that "the fact that masochism is disapproved of when stressful athletic activity and religious martyrdom are not is an interesting example of the way sex is made special case in our society".[53] It is certainly difficult to dismiss Califia's rationale, but his comments force the reader to consider what "goal" Townsend is attempting to achieve in her conscious simulation of porn performance. Indeed, for even though the narrator clearly enjoys sex, it is difficult to understand why her sexual veracity perpetually translates into conforming to the porn paradigm of sexual practices, calling to mind Dines' critical summation of female porn performers: "Even though these women love to be fucked, they seem to have no sexual imagination of their own: what they want always mirrors what the man wants."[54]

In forcing its stars to enact an unimaginative nymphomania, pornography presents women as lacking a sexual consciousness and valorises "sexual activity in which women are less than fully human".[55] Townsend's route to "empowerment" manifests itself through underscoring her nymphomania, and it becomes almost impossible for the reader to recognise her as an individual outside of sexual contexts. She amuses herself with the idea of her mother finding her "stash of lesbian anal porn" and

DOI: 10.1057/9781137326546

"twenty-four-carat gold-plated glass dildos",[56] and consequently (like the reader) perceiving her daughter as a nymphomaniac, collapsing gender transgression and sexual empowerment into the same space. Yet, rather than an authentic expression of female desire and selfhood, this transgression is entirely performative, evident in sexual exchanges that are disconnected from emotional intimacy. Townsend's sexual desire is expressed through a simulacrum of porn encounters, and we witness mutual masturbation sessions between her and her lover where "seeing him explode all over himself was one of the horniest things [she] had ever seen".[57] The interdependency of male ejaculation and female pleasure is significant, and Simon Hardy identifies the "money shot" (capturing the moment of external ejaculation) as "the ultimate distinguishing marker between private sex and porn performance", for it requires the sacrifice of what many people would consider to be "the crucial moment of tactile, inter-bodily pleasure in exchange for the visible, outward signification of pleasure".[58] In collapsing into the same ideological parameters the "authentic" tactile pleasures of participation and "inauthentic" pleasure derived from the visual objectification of sex acts, Townsend's memoir is demonstrative of the obscuring of the real and the representational[59] enacted by the consumption of pornography.

Conflations of the distinction between authenticity and performance are not reserved to Townsend's memoir. In Sienna Lewis' memoir, the narrator's description of sexual intercourse is remarkably concordant with porn sex: "This time I crouched on all fours with him behind me, rocking and slapping himself against my behind, one hand teasing my clit until I came, then turned, stripped the condom off him and took him into my mouth again. Just before he came I pulled back so he spurted all over my breasts and belly."[60] Similarly, in Suzanne Portnoy's *The Not So Invisible Woman* (2008), sexual fantasy is restricted to the porn paradigm: "My ultimate doctor fantasy is actually a threesome, with a hot male doctor and a sexy female nurse. I'm lying helpless on an examination table with my legs in stirrups, and a female nurse with great tits and a low-cut uniform is massaging my clit."[61] And in Toni Bentley's memoir, group sex is positioned not as a site of reciprocal pleasure but one of phallic worship: "She and I gathered like good girlfriends around his cock, which was hard, big, and beautiful. Four hands, two mouths. Every few minutes the Young Man raised his head to look down at the scene of angels praying together over his vertical altar."[62] Such reiterations of the formulas of porn sex are common in contemporary women's memoirs, yet what is perhaps most striking is the centralisation of less-mainstream erotic practices.

Krissy Kneen's narrator consumes pornography that features several "fisting" scenes, and despite wondering "if the process was damaging [the actress] in some way" she finds herself "coming back to the idea repeatedly", leading to "several failed attempts at a similar scenario".[63] Kneen's narrator does not explain nor appear to understand why she is imitating scenes from porn, nor does she express any pleasure during these reenactments, forcing the reader to conclude that she is merely capitulating to the pornography that invades her personal life. Belle de Jour's *The Intimate Adventures of a London Call Girl* (2005), provides a similar explanation for the current popularity of anal sex in women's intimate relationships. The narrator recalls the 1970s when "big-name porn stars didn't go there, when no one said it out loud", and "when the only people who made regular trips up the poop chute were gay men and prostate examiners". She continues to claim that the porn taboo of heterosexual anal sex served to mirror the social taboo, for in the 1970s a man "who suggested his wife grab her ankles and take it like a choirboy was probably courting divorce".[64] Now, in the 21st century, the narrator states that "anal sex is the new black" due to the "amateurisation of everything"[65] related to sexual practices. Such is the prolificacy of this pattern of porn simulation that real experiences of authentic sexual pleasure are now treated as somehow unusual and even anomalous, with Quan's prostitute-narrator admitting that she "shuddered hard" during a paid-sex encounter but "pulled away, slightly ashamed of this orgasm".[66] Quan's orgasm disrupts the male-dominated space of sexual encounters, and therefore disrupts her ability to perform as a porn star conforming to male desires. The manner in which the male-dominated aesthetics of pornography have become the identifying marker of contemporary sexual encounters will be the subject of the next section of this chapter.

The aesthetics of pornography

Simon Hardy notes that "the use of female authorship and first-person narration is clearly one strategy by which the pornographic genre as a whole, within which we may now include women's erotic memoirs, attempts to invoke the *real*, and close its distance as a representational practice from the empirical reality of its object."[67] Hardy continues to

DOI: 10.1057/9781137326546

claim that male produced pornography, from "Renaissance dialogues and erotic novels of the eighteenth century" to "readers' letters and stories sent in to porn magazines" frequently adopts the voice of the female to signal authenticity. The implication is that female accounts of sexuality are often perceived, especially by a male audience, as accurate and representational accounts of true sexual desire. The distinction could also be made between "erotica" and "porn" more discursively; the belief that "erotica" is an inscription of authentic female desire and "porn" of male-produced sexual fantasy. Yet, so far in this chapter, we have witnessed how the sexual practices documented in contemporary women's memoirs are complicit with the male-dominated porn paradigm of sexual exchanges. Sienna Lewis' memoir demonstrates, in particular, how everyday sexual encounters have become colonised by the gender and aesthetic hierarchies of pornography. In one notable sex scene, foreplay manifests itself not through the mutual kissing and touching of two partners, but through the narrator viewing "pictures of girls in short skirts with bare arses being spanked and slapped" until her lover "pushed his way inside [her] and fucked [her]".[68] What this incident demonstrates is not only the manner in which intimacy has been transformed by the popularisation of pornographic media culture, but also how female desire is now positioned as dependant on adhering to the aesthetics of pornography through a greater focalisation on the anatomies of men and women.

The prevalence of this pattern – which is apparent in all of the memoirs discussed in this book – is perhaps not surprising if we place popular memoirs in a postfeminist frame of reference, and especially if we define postfeminism as "indicative of a 'post-traditional' era characterised by dramatic changes in basic social relationships, role stereotyping and conceptions of agency".[69] The pattern of women's sexual desire reconfigured as similar to male desire, rather than oppositional is both recurring and distinct in the majority of the memoirs. Townsend confesses: "forget all this stuff about women not being visual, I prefer my porn to have minimal storylines and maximum action!"[70] Reflecting on her "sexual hard-wiring", Townsend comments on having "always felt like a freak" for, in opposition to popular constructions of female sexuality activated by emotional intimacy, she is "very visual when it comes to sex", leading to numerous textual accounts of the importance of bodily objectification in her experience of desire: "Seeing JP step out of the shower, or even bend over to take out the washing, and catching a sideways sliver of toned

DOI: 10.1057/9781137326546

stomach or the ripple in his calves and curve of his ass as he pulls out the whites sends me into a frenzy."[71] However, while mass-market memoirs such as Townsend's place onus on a sexual subjectivity activated by male objectification, literary memoirs by contrast place onus on the body as an aesthetic form to be viewed as an object of beauty.

In *The Sexual Life of Catherine M.*, Millet observes that "a dick which is constantly exposed demands to be looked at", and even though there is the recognition that objectification "provokes sexual excitement" the emphasis remains focused on describing the "smooth monolithic contours" of the penis, "the foreskin that you can play back and forth, uncovering the glans like a great bubble forming on the surface of soapy water"; a process that "elicits a more subtle sensuality"[72] in counterpoint to the "frenzy" described by Townsend. This perspective is also apparent in Melissa P.'s memoir, in which the narrator "studied the curves" of her lover's back and "marvelled at them",[73] while Bentley likewise describes her lover in neo-classical terms as "Michelangelo's *David*, his chest is broad, his skin is smooth, his hands are huge, his face beatific".[74] For the authors of literary memoirs, then, the process of objectification is an aesthetic one as much as sexual, marking the literary memoir as the domain of erotica where the artistry of the body is of paramount importance. In their appropriation of the male lens, these memoirs are also more politically aware compared to mass-market memoirs, with authors like Melissa P. noting that she watches her lover "masturbate as if [she] had assumed a male gaze".[75] The third-wave feminist sensibility of occupying the male space ensures that literary memoirs stand in counterpoint to mass-market memoirs, where the subjectivity of pleasure is, in itself, positioned as a postfeminist strategy of self-actualisation.

Indeed, mass market memoirs often position female (self)objectification, and the pleasure it accords, as a feminist strategy that cannot be subjected to the same critiques compared to the cornerstone site of feminist protest: the objectification of women by men. In Abby Lee's *Girl with a One Track Mind* (2006), arousal is generated by not only viewing "a handsome man sitting with his legs splayed apart" on the train but also by "observing the breast jiggle of a buxom woman as she ran for the bus".[76] Similar to Townsend's aforementioned admission that she is "very visual when it comes to sex", Abby Lee concedes that she views women's bodies "like any straight man", involving "looking at her breasts and imagining them in [her] mouth".[77] At one particularly significant moment in her memoir, Lee sees a beautiful woman dancing in a bar,

DOI: 10.1057/9781137326546

and proceeds to check the "sumptuous arse over which she was wearing a body-hugging wrap dress and absolutely no underwear". Lee finds that she "couldn't stop staring at her bum; it was like a siren, calling squeeze me, slap me".[78]

The objectification of the bodies of women by women, and the pleasure it affords, remains a prominent theme, and the aesthetics of porn are further centralised in the manner in which the female body is itemised. In *Affection*, Krissy Kneen's narrator masturbates while "dreaming of her labia or her breasts or her hair, but [...] never the whole person",[79] demonstrating how female desire is inseparable from the visualisation and concomitant dissection of the anatomies of other women. Yet, what is perhaps especially interesting is the increasing dominance of the role of one's own body in the construction of female desire. Popular women's memoirs contain many elements that ostensibly parallel second-wave feminist critiques of pornography in which "women are sexual objects and men are sexual subjects",[80] yet they equally construct a female subjectivity that is thoroughly postfeminist by resituating sexual objectification as entirely self-willed. Even though many cultural commentators such as Ariel Levy reject this form of postfeminist assertion, perceiving it to be nothing more than a hegemonic internalisation of the values of the increasingly pervasive sex industry, others position self-objectification as a means of enacting not only female pleasure but, more significantly, female agency. Challenging the objectification of women remains a core tenet of contemporary feminist politics – one only has to look towards Naomi Wolf's *The Beauty Myth* (1991) as evidence of the third-wave's interest in this form of media representation – yet many third-wave feminists have also come to position self-objectification as empowering.

Kathy Myers calls to mind – only to then refute – traditional anti-representation perspectives, stating that "feminist critiques of the representation of women hinge on the assumption that it is the act of representation or objectification itself which degrades women, reducing them to the status of objects to be 'visually' or 'literally' consumed." Myers continues to suggest that this position functions to "deny women the right to represent their own sexuality" and "side-steps the whole issue of female sexual pleasure", concluding that "questions of representation and of pleasure cannot be separated".[81] From this perspective, any analysis of pornography which focuses solely on its content is in danger of falling into a form of reductive essentialism, and ignores the fact that it is not the representation of female sexuality that is inherently patriarchal, but

DOI: 10.1057/9781137326546

rather the conditions and contexts that produce these representations. Popular women's memoirs support this view, and many position self-representation – and the sexual self-awareness it accords – as central to female sexual pleasure. Even though Krissy Kneen's memoir replicates the porn paradigm, she positions the visual presentation of her own body as of paramount importance, even more so than the tactile experience of sex. After placing her fist inside her vagina, Kneen confesses: "the image reflected back at me when he held up a little mirror, tipped me over the edge and after that I had no interest in continuing."[82]

The image of the sexual self reflected in a mirror recurs in a number of memoirs. In Melissa P.'s, the narrator comments that "the pleasure of observing me is so intense and powerful that it immediately turns physical",[83] an experience conveyed by Toni Bentley through the analogy of ballet dancing:

> Ballet dancing is learned in front of a mirror. Hours and hours and hours and hours in front of a mirror. As a little girl, as a serious student, and then as a professional adult in both classes and rehearsals, I learned that every arch of the foot, every glance of the eye, every angle of the arm, every turn of the leg, every smile, every grimace, every strain is simultaneously performed and witnessed by one's self, the nebulous entity called consciousness. One becomes both subject and object.[84]

Even in memoirs that do not feature the motif of the mirror image, the recognition of an active sexual agency is premised on an investment in the objectification of oneself. In Abby Lee's memoir, the author describes a dress that "clings to every curve on [her] body", a dress that accentuates her figure and displays her breasts "in all their glory, proudly cupping them as if they were the firmest, roundest bosoms in all the world".[85] The narrator admits that it is "the sight of the curve of [her] arse against the material" that "makes [her] want to touch [herself]",[86] demonstrating how sexual desire is generated by visual and psychological factors rather than tactile. Portnoy's memoir further supports this position, with the narrator declaring: "having a camera aimed at me brought out my exhibitionist tendencies. I found the whole thing a big turn-on."[87] Likewise, Grandes' narrator concedes that masturbating in front of her lover has the effect of not only "arousing him from a distance" but leads to "a terrible urge to go over and touch him".[88]

What these examples indicate is that the ability to subjectively experience sexual pleasure is often dependent upon either a visual or an

DOI: 10.1057/9781137326546

imaginative affirmation of oneself as a desirable object. In the words of Melissa P., the purpose of "the corset, black silk with lace and ribbons" is to make her body "too curvaceous and buttery for men to refrain from releasing their bestiality",[89] situating objectification as central to male and female experiences of sexual desire. While Townsend admits that the role of objectification in the creation of sexual desire has been "honed through years of rifling through airbrushed magazines and lesbian porn",[90] and while Lee concedes that lingerie perpetuates "the same sexist, objectified view of femaleness that was shoved down [her] throat by the cover of every magazine",[91] both authors ultimately affirm the centrality of visual objectification to sexual desire and female empowerment. In postfeminist culture, it is easy to understand why many authors situate the objectification of male and female bodies as liberating, for in certain situations women who are viewed as sexually desirable are certainly able to exert power over some men. Yet, as Robert Jensen observes, women's power in those moments "does not automatically extend into power in the wider world of business or politics",[92] and the contemporary obsession with sexual representation could easily be attributed not to empowerment, but rather to the global dominance of a media-saturated, celebrity-obsessed cultural climate in which "putting oneself into the frame of representation is becoming a means of existential assertion".[93]

This chapter has explored the impact of pornography on contemporary women's memoirs, raising questions concerning how the popularisation of the sex industry may impact on the aesthetic notions and sexual values of female-authored popular narratives. We have discovered that despite the feminist potential of the memoir as a literary form, the mass-market texts discussed in this chapter can only be positioned in a postfeminist frame of reference in which empowerment is conditional on a number of limiting factors. Through analysing the memoirs' depiction of sexual practices, it has been demonstrated that while the texts reflect the aesthetic paradigm of male-produced pornography, the authors/narrators of the memoirs attempt to reconfigure this paradigm as empowering to female sexual agency. This is enacted through accentuating the objectification of the bodies of women by women, most conspicuously in terms of the itemisation of the female body. Through contesting the notion that the visual objectification of the female body is inherently patriarchal, contemporary erotic memoirs position self-representation, and the sexual self-awareness it accords, as central to female sexual

DOI: 10.1057/9781137326546

pleasure, demonstrating how sexual desire is generated by visual and psychological factors rather than tactile. The memoirs inhabit a space that is both progressive and regressive – a challenge to and an affirmation of conventional femininity – the former by forcefully expressing female sexual desire in their (visual) consumption of male and female bodies, and the latter by adhering to the conventions of male-produced pornography. While scholars like Kathy Myers have commented that "questions of representation and of pleasure cannot be separated, and that a feminist erotica could examine the nature of this relationship",[94] and while it is clear that contemporary women's memoirs are framed as liberatory, it remains difficult to deny that they have yet to cast off, and rather continue to celebrate, the spectre of male domination.

Notes

1   Susanna Paasonen, "Good Amateurs: Erotica Writing and Notions of Quality" in *Porn.com: Making Sense of Online Pornography*, ed. Feona Attwood (New York: Peter Lang, 2010), 150.

2   Ibid., 139.

3   Dana Wilson-Kovacs, "Some Texts Do It Better: Women, Sexually Explicit Texts and the Everyday" in *Mainstreaming Sex: The Sexualisation of Western Cultures*, ed. Feona Attwood (London: I.B. Tauris, 2009), 148.

4   Clarissa Smith, *One for the Girls!: The Pleasures and Practices of Reading Women's Porn* (Bristol: Intellect Books, 2007), 9.

5   Naomi Wolf, *Promiscuities: A Secret History of Female Desire* (London: Vintage, 1998), 3.

6   Jennifer Baumgardner and Amy Richards, *Manifesta: Young Women, Feminism and the Future* (New York: Farrar, Straus and Giroux, 2010 [2000]), 20.

7   Wolf, *Promiscuities*, 5.

8   Feona Attwood, "Porn Studies: From Social Problem to Cultural Practice" in *Porn.com: Making Sense of Online Pornography*, ed. Feona Attwood (New York: Peter Lang, 2010), 1.

9   Ibid.

10   Jeffrey Weeks, *Sexuality* (London and New York: Routledge, 2003), 125.

11   Mariana Valverde, "Pornography: Not for Men Only" in *Sexual Lives: A Reader on the Theories and Realities of Human Sexualities*, eds Betsy Crane and Robert Heasley (New York: McGraw-Hill, 2003), 467.

12   Ibid., 470.

13   Lynne Segal, *Is the Future Female?:Troubled Thoughts on Contemporary Feminism* (London: Virago, 1987), 105.

DOI: 10.1057/9781137326546

14   Pat Califia, "Feminism and Sadomasochism" in *Feminism and Sexuality: A Reader*, eds Stevi Jackson and Sue Scott (Edinburgh: Edinburgh University Press, 1996), 236.

15   Walter, *Living Dolls*, 102.

16   Linda Williams, *Hard Core: Power, Pleasure and the "Frenzy of the Visible"* (London: Pandora Press, 1991), 22.

17   Gail Dines, *Pornland: How Porn Has Hijacked Our Sexuality* (Boston, MA: Beacon Press, 2010), 34.

18   Ibid.

19   Ibid., 104–105.

20   Katherine N. Kinnick, "Pushing the Envelope: The Role of the Mass Media in the Mainstreaming of Pornography" in *Pop-Porn: Pornography in American Culture*, eds M.J. Bishop and A.C. Hall (Westport, CT: Praeger Publishers, 2007), 9.

21   Ibid., 22.

22   Mardia J. Bishop, "The Making of a Pre-Pubescent Porn Star: Contemporary Fashion for Elementary School Girls" in *Pop-Porn: Pornography in American Culture*, eds M.J. Bishop and A.C. Hall, (Westport, CT: Praeger Publishers, 2007), 54.

23   Natasha Walter, *Living Dolls: The Return of Sexism* (London: Virago, 2010), 105.

24   Stephanie Genz and Benjamin Brabon, *Postfeminism: Cultural Texts and Theories* (Edinburgh: Edinburgh University Press, 2009), 92.

25   Imelda Whelehan, *Overloaded: Popular Culture and the Future of Feminism* (London: The Women's Press, 2000), 37.

26   Catherine Townsend, *Sleeping Around: Secrets of a Sexual Adventuress* (London: John Murray, 2007), 134.

27   Walter, *Living Dolls*, 109.

28   Toni Bentley, *The Surrender: An Erotic Memoir* (London: Harper Perennial, 2006), 122.

29   Ibid., 121.

30   Tracy Quan, *Diary of a Married Call Girl* (London: Harper Perennial, 2006 [2005]), 44.

31   Ibid., 115.

32   Genz and Brabon, *Postfeminism: Cultural Texts and Theories*, 80.

33   Quan, *Diary of a Married Call Girl*, 44.

34   Sienna Lewis, *Intimate Adventures of an Office Girl* (London: Avon Books, 2009), 89.

35   Ibid.

36   Tracy Quan, *Diary of a Manhattan Call Girl* (London: Harper Perennial, 2005 [2001]), 30.

37   Krissy Kneen, *Affection: An Erotic Memoir* (Berkeley, California: Seal Press, 2010), 55.

DOI: 10.1057/9781137326546

38 Melissa P., *One Hundred Strokes of the Brush before Bed*, trans. Lawrence Venuti (London: Serpent's Tail, 2004), 56.

39 Dawn Porter, *Diaries of an Internet Lover* (London: Virgin Books, 2006), 6.

40 Ibid., 108.

41 Suzanne Portnoy, *The Butcher, the Baker, the Candlestick Maker* (London: Virgin Books, 2006), 157.

42 Townsend, *Sleeping Around*, 134.

43 Dines, *Pornland*, xvii.

44 Ibid., 108.

45 Catherine Townsend, *Breaking the Rules: Confessions of a Bad Girl* (London: John Murray, 2008), 24.

46 Ibid., 27.

47 Shelley Budgeon, "Fashion Magazine Advertising: Constructing Femininity in the 'Postfeminist' Era" in *Gender and Utopia in Advertising: A Critical Reader*, eds Luigi Manca and Alessandra Manda (Lisle, IL: Procopian Press, 1994), 66.

48 Robert Jensen, *Getting Off: Pornography and the End of Masculinity* (Cambridge, MA: South End Press, 2007), 62.

49 Ibid., 56.

50 Townsend, *Breaking the Rules*, 167.

51 Angela McRobbie, *The Aftermath of Feminism: Gender, Culture and Social Change* (London: Sage, 2009), 17.

52 Ibid., 18.

53 Califia, "Feminism and Sadomasochism", 234.

54 Dines, *Pornland*, xxiii.

55 Ibid., 61.

56 Townsend, *Breaking the Rules*, 30.

57 Ibid., 54.

58 Simon Hardy, "The New Pornographies: Representation or Reality?" in *Mainstreaming Sex: The Sexualization of Western Cultures*, ed. Feona Attwood (London: I.B. Tauris, 2009), 10.

59 Attwood, "Porn Studies", 6.

60 Lewis, *Intimate Adventures of an Office Girl*, 47.

61 Suzanne Portnoy, *The Not So Invisible Woman* (London: Virgin Books, 2008), 8.

62 Bentley, *The Surrender*, 37.

63 Kneen, *Affection*, 148.

64 Belle de Jour, *The Intimate Adventures of a London Call Girl* (London: Phoenix, 2005), 107.

65 Ibid.

66 Quan, *Diary of a Married Call Girl*, 113.

67 Hardy, "The New Pornographies", 7.

68 Lewis, *Intimate Adventures of an Office Girl*, 75.

DOI: 10.1057/9781137326546

69 Genz and Brabon, *Postfeminism: Cultural Texts and Theories*, 1.
70 Townsend, *Breaking the Rules,* 166.
71 Ibid., 191.
72 Catherine Millet, *The Sexual Life of Catherine M.*, trans. Adriana Hunter (London: Corgi Books, 2003 [2002]), 18.
73 Melissa P., *One Hundred Strokes*, 20.
74 Bentley, *The Surrender*, 161.
75 Melissa P., *One Hundred Strokes*, 48.
76 Abby Lee, *Girl with a One Track Mind: Confessions of the Seductress Next Door* (London: Ebury Press, 2006), 32.
77 Ibid., 84.
78 Ibid., 79.
79 Kneen, *Affection*, 199.
80 Jensen, *Getting Off*, 64.
81 Kathy Myers, "Towards a Feminist Erotica" in *Sexual Lives: A Reader on the Theories and Realities of Human Sexuality*, eds Betsy Crane and Robert Heasley (New York: McGraw-Hill, 2003), 485.
82 Kneen, *Affection*, 149.
83 Melissa P., *One Hundred Strokes*, 2.
84 Bentley, *The Surrender*, 20.
85 Lee, *Girl with a One Track Mind*, 163.
86 Ibid., 39.
87 Portnoy, *The Butcher*, 59.
88 Almudena Grandes, *The Ages of Lulu*, trans. S. Soto (London: Phoenix, 2005 [1993]), 128.
89 Melissa P., *One Hundred Strokes*, 67.
90 Townsend, *Breaking the Rules*, 116.
91 Lee, *Girl with a One Track Mind*, 38.
92 Jensen, *Getting Off*, 174.
93 Paasonen, "Good Amateurs", 150.
94 Myers, "Towards a Feminist Erotica", 485.

DOI: 10.1057/9781137326546

4
Transgression

Abstract: *This chapter focuses on how women's erotic memoirs position sexual desire as constitutionally subversive, and therefore inherently difficult to place in harmonious agreement with any political framework. While recognising that sexual experiences are unavoidably political as powerful agents for subverting social norms and institutional values, the chapter argues that sexual desire and behaviour is often resistant to "traditional" or "politically correct" feminist politics. As such, it demonstrates how many contemporary erotic memoirs position violence – both received and enacted – as a necessary and even desired component of sexual practice, locating the memoirs' attitudes to sexual violence in both postfeminist culture and third-wave feminist ideology.*

Gwynne, Joel. *Erotic Memoirs and Postfeminism: The Politics of Pleasure*. Basingstoke: Palgrave Macmillan, 2013.
DOI: 10.1057/9781137326546.

Reflecting on the sources of sexual anxiety and sexual taboo, Michael Warner decrees that "sex is an occasion for losing control, for merging one's consciousness with the lower orders of animal desire and sensation, for raw confrontations of power and demand".[1] In sexuality resides always the potential for both affirmative and transgressive experiences, concordant with the status of sex as a domain of restriction, repression and danger, as much as exploration, pleasure and agency. Warner continues to observe that sexuality is inherently unpredictable, for "the possibility of abject shame is never entirely out of the picture".[2] Gayle Rubin comments that, precisely for this reason, "sex is presumed guilty until proven innocent", and continues to assert that "virtually all erotic behavior is considered bad unless a specific reason to exempt it has been established".[3] The most common reasons for "excusing" sex – marriage, reproduction and romantic love – almost certainly position sexual experience as inextricable from narratives of cultural production. To be sexually active outside of society's carefully enunciated moral parameters is often a mark of not only social transgression but, more significantly, political insubordination. The potential social consequences of sexual activity, and the spectre of societal condemnation, haunts all aspects of sexual conduct.

Sexuality operates within a political and social framework that is both affirmative and prohibitive. Commenting on the manner in which modern Western societies appraise sexuality according to a hierarchical system of sexual values, Rubin states that "marital, reproductive heterosexuals are alone at the top of the erotic pyramid", while "the most despised sexual castes" range from transsexuals, transvestites, fetishists, sadomasochists, and sex workers to "the lowliest of all, those whose eroticism transgresses generational boundaries".[4] Even in contexts where sex is socially sanctioned, namely heterosexual marital relationships, sexuality remains, for many, a subject that is emotive and taboo, largely due to the fact that Western cultures often perceive sex as a dangerous, destructive, negative force. Rubin has termed the dominance of this attitude as "sex negativity", locating its emergence in Christian doctrine which holds that sex is inherently sinful, and can only be redeemed if "performed within marriage for procreative purposes", and if the "pleasurable aspects are not enjoyed too much", notions that have "now acquired a life of their own and no longer depend solely on religion for their perseverance".[5] Attitudes that have historically positioned sexual activity as sinful, immoral or dangerous to one's health have been disseminated through

DOI: 10.1057/9781137326546

a variety of institutions, yet, Jeffrey Weeks observes that it is only in the late-20th century that these stories gained a mass audience, narratives that are implicated in moral and political change and "hold the potential for radical transformations of the social order".[6]

Therein resides the transgressive potential of erotic memoirs, especially if we consider the historical suppression of female sexuality and the current restriction of female desire to zones protected and privileged in culture, specifically marriage and the nuclear family. Carol Vance asserts that even though the boundaries of the "safe zone" have been reconceptualised to include "relatively respectable forms of unmarried and non-procreative heterosexuality", it remains the case that "gross and public departures" from normative sexuality, such as lesbianism, promiscuity or non-traditional heterosexuality, "still invite – and are thought to justify – violation".[7] It is a consequence of this culture of fear towards, and of, female sexuality that women come to experience their own sexual impulses as dangerous. This awareness of the dangers of sexuality is inevitably caused by patriarchy, yet even beyond patriarchy – a problematic speculative space, I admit – there remains an entire erotic tradition that identifies and conceptualises sexuality and sexual desire as inherently transgressive. As Clarissa Smith observes, to experience the erotic "involves the sense of an interior self, a self that is always vulnerable to invasion from the outside – that defends itself yet longs for the invasion", locating sexuality as inherently masochistic: "Masochism lends itself to all erotic experience in this sense, since it involves the capacity to be shattered into joy or *jouissance* by an extreme pleasure that is also intense suffering."[8] If conceptualised in this manner, the erotic is dangerous because it evokes contradictory impulses – pleasure and pain; submission and subordination – that are often difficult to rationalise, contain and compartmentalise. The transgressive potential of sexual desire lies in its unpredictability and resistance to both the rational mind and the pragmatic and moral codes that organise societies.

This chapter evaluates how popular women's memoirs position female sexual desire as constitutionally transgressive, and aims to answer the following questions: How do contemporary memoirs situate sexual desire as necessarily violent, and how is this violence embraced? How do the memoirs perceive the uncontainability of sexual desire as a powerful agent for subverting social norms and institutional values? How do they serve to destigmatise and normalise taboo sexual identities and behaviours commonly perceived to be deviant? And finally, how should

DOI: 10.1057/9781137326546

we locate sexually transgressive practices in the context of postfeminist culture and third-wave feminism, and are these practices always empowering? While popular women's memoirs emphatically document transgression as an emergent script of postfeminist femininity, this chapter seeks to expose the reactionary nature of this ostensible subversion of traditional femininity.

Reconceptualising sexual violence: fantasy and practice

At the height of the second-wave "sex wars", a vocal minority of prominent feminists contested all manifestations of sexual violence, and refused to make a distinction between the fantasy of coercion and its material embodiment. This assumption was central to debates surrounding pornography in the 1980s. In Andrea Dworkin's words, "Pornography is the material means of sexualizing inequality; and that is why pornography is a central practice in the subordination of women."[9] In Dworkin's analysis, as well as teaching women their place as whores, pornography also serves as ubiquitous propaganda, acting as a catalyst to acts of male violence against women. This is precisely why second-wave feminist research predominantly focused on experiences of sexual violence, and established that "rape involves the sexualization of power" and the "fusing in men's imaginations of sexual pleasure with domination and control".[10] More recently, Gail Dines has summarised the complexities of this argument: "How porn is implicated in rape is complex and multilayered. Clearly, not all men who use porn rape, but what porn does is create what some feminists call a 'rape culture' by normalizing, legitimizing, and condoning violence against women."[11] Understood in this context, all sexual violence, whether real, performed or imagined, is catastrophically detrimental. Yet, in a comment that is perhaps emblematic of third-wave sex-positive feminism, Becky McLaughlin declares: "I have yet to decide the ramifications of admitting that one might want (at least in one's imagination) to be treated like an errant Barbie doll. That one might like being victimised by a group of scantily clad Belgian boys. That one might get a libidinal charge out of gazing at a wounded body."[12]

The desire to receive and enact violence, in both sexual fantasy and sexual practice, is now well-documented in many aspects of mass and high culture. The diversity of sexual economies and practices represented

DOI: 10.1057/9781137326546

in the mainstream media is paralleled by the diversity of attitudes to minority sexualities in contemporary feminist scholarship. In spite of, and in response to, second-wave contestation of sexual violence, many third-wave feminists have continued to emphasise the crucial distinctions between fantasy and reality. Chris Daley acknowledges that while "the real violence of self-mutilation and the simulated violence of erotic spanking may seem part of the same patriarchal power structure that leads women to despise our bodies and identities", it is crucial to distinguish between "*permanence* and *pretense, masochism* and *playful masquerade*" (emphasis in original).[13] Applying this idea to the subject of violent sexual fantasies, Naomi Wolf makes a similar point, arguing that what "women fantasize about may or may not shed light on what they want in real life",[14] while Lynne Segal offers a more critical dissection of the relationship between fantasy and reality: "If heterosexual contact really is a type of sexual violence, then feminists' own 'perverse' masochistic fantasies can seem to make some sense as the only way that women have learned to cope with men's coercive sexuality."[15]

Segal tentatively suggests that sexual fantasies are rather "like the nightmares of shell-shocked soldiers who relive the experience of battle to help them cope with it in future",[16] yet this position is implicitly challenged by the narrator of Catherine Millet's *The Sexual Life of Catherine M.*:

> There are major structural similarities between situations I have lived and those I have imagined, even though I have never actively chosen to reproduce the latter in my life, and the details of what I have lived have had little part in nourishing my imaginings. Perhaps I should just assume that the fantasies forged in my earliest youth predisposed me to widely diverse experiences. Having never felt ashamed of these fantasies, and having reworked and embellished them rather than trying to bury them, they offered no opposition to what was real but rather a sort of mesh through which real-life situations that other people might have found outrageous struck me as quite normal.[17]

For Millet, sexual fantasy precedes sexual practice, and is not a means by which women "cope" with men's coercive sexuality, but rather the opposite: an experience that enables women to enjoy a diversity of sexual experiences in later life, including those which are violent. Even though Segal proposes that women's sexual fantasies are protectionist, she also proceeds to note that, as exemplified by Millet, women do nevertheless often take great pleasure in coercive fantasy, concluding that "neither

DOI: 10.1057/9781137326546

women's nor men's sexual fantasies reflect simply the reality of male dominance and misogyny", but rather "draw upon all manner of infantile sexual wishes".[18] Scholars such as Daley and Segal are representative of a movement towards a greater acceptance of sexual coercion in private feminist play, and arguments for the pleasures of sadomasochism (S/M) in particular have become noticeably vocal over the past two decades. S/M practitioners and scholars stress the consensual nature of S/M experiences, and reject the pathologising impulses of psychoanalytic and psychiatric accounts. Like Daley, they challenge the notion that S/M is based on patriarchal power structures, asserting that while the social structures of power that typify patriarchy are irrefutably institutionalised and rigid, the sexual practice of S/M remains a fluid and pluralised relation.[19] Linda Williams has highlighted how this fluid relationship operates in real-world encounters, and often serves to complicate any distinct binary of oppression and subordination: "The predominant desire in both male and female sadomasochism is apparently to be dominated rather than to dominate, although [...] these terms are themselves complicated, for in a sense the dominated seeks indirectly to dominate as well."[20]

The perspectives of Daley and Williams function to reenvision the manner in which S/M is viewed in popular culture as "the perverse abuse by male sadists of female masochists".[21] When sexual coercion features as a component of any sexual practice, it is often assumed that such coercion emerges as a result of "false consciousness"; women eroticising the conditions of their own oppression. Feminism has placed many women under great pressure to deny aspects of their sexuality that appear counterproductive to feminist politics. As Merri Lisa Johnson has noted, "being a proper and good feminist" involves submitting to political pressures that embrace the perspective that "connecting sex and death devalues the erotic" and "condones and fetishizes the brutalized female body", a position that is antithetical to her "real response" to sexual domination: "I want someone to fuck the shit out of me".[22] Johnson proceeds to offer an explanation of why many women who self-identify as feminists would perhaps "want to be fucked hard, held down, thrown against walls", stating that "as feminists, we've learned to critique [male aggression], we know there's something wrong with it, it has been removed to the space of transgression, that which we are not supposed to want".[23] Even though many feminists would perhaps note the dangerous implications of Johnson's position – if the same principles were applied to all aspects of women's experience then feminist movements

DOI: 10.1057/9781137326546

would surely collapse – her position is refreshingly honest and receptive to the contrariness and diversity that demarcates sexual experience and complicates the "personal is political".

The desire to be the recipient of sexual violence and abuse is most commonly represented in the form of sexual fantasy. In Melissa P's *One Hundred Strokes of the Brush Before Bed* (2004), the author describes a friend who "touches herself, and she said when she does it she likes to imagine she's being possessed by a man, hard, violently, as if she were going to be hurt".[24] In Krissy Kneen's *Affection: An Erotic Memoir* (2010), masturbation is accompanied by "a repertoire of lascivious images"[25] borrowed from banned books, and the narrator's dreams of sexual domination are imbued with the threat of violence: "In the dream they circled me and I felt their shadows dark and cold like sharks brushing against my legs. My fear silenced me [...] I was acutely aware of each of these sensations and if I woke before the first man had finished with me and zipped up, stepping aside for another man to take his place, then I would be disappointed."[26] The threat of violence in sexual fantasy highlighted by Melissa P. and Kneen can be paralleled with sexual fantasies in which pleasure is predicated on actual violence. Suzanne Portnoy's narrator describes "being gang-banged" as a "pretty run-of-the-mill"[27] fantasy, and Belle de Jour's imagines working as "a testing engineer for an office supplies manufacturer, and that the job involved covering [her] inner thighs with bulldog clips as someone screwed [her] vigorously".[28]

The dominance of abusive sexual fantasies in popular women's memoirs, whether imagined or as an appendage to real sexual encounters, can perhaps be explained by Michael Warner's observation that while many sexual practices appear "innocently moral, consistent with nature and health", it is always necessary to examine "the premises of one's morality", for what "looks like crime might be harmless difference", and what "looks like pathology might be a rival form of health, or a higher tolerance of stress".[29] Moving beyond the realms of sexual fantasy, the majority of the memoirs discussed in this book pursue Warner's morally plural trajectory, largely in their configuration of sex as an experience that is inherently and necessarily violent. This is most explicitly evident in literary memoirs, and in Melissa P's the narrator notes the transformation of her lover from "a polite, well-bred young man to a coarse, vulgar beast"[30] when overcome with desire. Yet, crucially, she does not construct this in negative terms. On the contrary, the narrator concedes: "Violence kills me, wears me down, dirties me, and feeds on me, but with

DOI: 10.1057/9781137326546

and for it I survive, I feed on it."[31] Similarly, in Almudena Grandes' *The Ages of Lulu* (1993), the narrator describes a sexual encounter in which all her "expectations had been fulfilled" by men who are described as "animals, delicious, brutal, sincere, violent, slaves to their greedy flesh, as wilful as small children, incapable of restraining the least desire",[32] and whose violence "added an irresistible note to the pleasure", setting off "an exquisitely brutal climax".[33] In contrast, the pleasure experienced by Catherine Millet's narrator lies not in the experience of sexual violence, but in surveying the aftermath of these encounters: "When I was left to rest, I would become aware that my vagina was gorged. It was a pleasure feeling its walls stiffened, heavy, slightly painful, in their own way bearing the imprint of all the members that had touched base there."[34]

Mass-market memoirs follow the same pattern, extolling acts of both material sexual violence and performative S/M as essential to positive sexual experiences for they subvert, or at least supplement, genital focused intercourse. Chris Daley has commented on the tendency among us all to defer "automatically to the culturally preferred genital-focused fuck",[35] despite the fact that sexual learning in adolescence centres around sexual play and exploration that is not genitally oriented. Linda Williams sees the transgression of S/M practices as manifested not in "the extremity of the violence enacted or endured for purposes of obtaining pleasure", but rather in the way that "violence, aggression and pain become vehicles for [...] staging dramas of suspense, supplication, abandon".[36] In Belle de Jour's *The Intimate Adventures of a London Call Girl* (2005), the narrator testifies to the drama of sex where arousal occurs, not from sexual action, but from the performance of violence: "I had too much to eat – when I went down on him, his member was too big and it choked me. I coughed up Meat Feast and Diet Coke on his thigh. His penis grew even harder. He pulled my hair until I cried as he masturbated on my tear- and vomit-covered face."[37] After a subsequent encounter in which violence occurs more explicitly – "He whipped me through a shirt, then topless, stopping only when I started to bleed" – the pleasure experienced by both parties is generated not by the violence of the encounter but the visual outcome: "After he spent his load on my face he held a mirror up. 'You are such a picture', he sighed. Eyes stinging with come, I half-opened my lids to see a red-cheeked girl squatting in a white-tiled bath. And he was right. It looked good. Not in a cover-of-*Glamour* way, mind. I smiled broadly."[38]

While many contemporary feminists would surely refuse to distinguish between "real" and "performative" sexual violence, the examples

DOI: 10.1057/9781137326546

from the memoirs can be understood as what scholars have termed "topping from the bottom", occasions where the ostensible subordinate "initiates and commands the sexual play" and where the lines between top and bottom, between exerting and submitting to power, conflate and dissolve. Applying this rationale to the examples discussed, it is the broad smile of de Jour that affirms her position as a woman in power, subverting any notion of the brutalised female body as a site of patriarchal subordination. The audience understands that there is never any doubt regarding the consensual nature of the narrator's violent encounters, and perhaps therein lies the problem for many feminist critics; the notion that women, like all individuals, do not always embrace the healthy and wholesome aspects of human experience. Analysing sexual encounters from nothing more than a perspective that focuses on the unequal gender binary of man/woman and domination/submission fails to take into account how the violence, and therefore the power, of sexual desire can function as politically and socially transgressive in disparate ways. This, then, is the subject of the next section of this chapter.

Sex, transgression and society

In *Promiscuities: A Secret History of Female Desire* (1998), Naomi Wolf recollects her own adolescent memories of awakening sexuality, and in doing so demarcates the relationship between sexual desire and other forms of social transgression: "We wanted the Irish boys precisely because they were considered 'unsuitable' for us [...] Because we were told they inhabited an erotic region outside the safe parameters of our community, we wanted them all the more."[39] In another recollection, Wolf recalls how her desire for Devin, a "foul-mouthed kid from a depressed country town", was entirely predicated on an awareness that their relationship would provoke those who chose to restrict her behaviour: "It was precisely because I knew Devin would wipe away my reputation among the authority figures in my life that I wanted him."[40] For Wolf, sexual transgression is clearly linked to gender subversion, aware that her desire to develop a sexual relationship with the town rebel is the most effective way to transgress all other restrictive codes of feminine behaviour. To be a female sexual transgressor is to vehemently reject many forms of social pressure that coerce women to perform femininity and which – especially in the case of adolescent girls – usually culminates in

DOI: 10.1057/9781137326546

subordination to male (parental) authority. Yet, even so, Wolf's desire to develop a relationship with Devin needs to be understood as much more than merely an attraction to the liberation attained through becoming an actively sexual teenage girl. Wolf recalls Devin's evolution from a boy who "wore a rotation of white T-shirts" and "kept his cigarettes rolled up in the sleeve", to a young man who eventually found work as a salesman, "a good job for the region", and confesses that a photo of him in his "jacket and necktie, and with the proud expression of a wage-earner" made her "heart sink".[41]

Wolf's recollection of the sadness evoked by Devin's transformation demonstrates that life progression – from social deviant, to social acceptance, to social success – often entails, in some way, losing one's spirit by repressing aspects of the self that society identifies as dangerous and a potential cause of social instability. In terms of sexual identities, it is sexual desire and sexual activity that are often positioned as aspects of human behaviour that create discord in society, as dangerous to notions of civilization and social decency. In popular women's memoirs, attempts to reconcile sexuality and societal conventions are fraught with complication. In Krissy Kneen's *Affection: An Erotic Memoir* (2010), the author's existential reflections attribute the problem of human existence to "the space between orgasms, the terrible chasm of daily life, the social imperatives, the pointless living".[42] Orgasm is positioned as a form of relief and catharsis from the monotony of existence, and while this may be interpreted as somewhat melodramatic many of the memoirs discussed in this book locate the exigencies of routine as antithetical to sexual pleasure. In Toni Bentley's *The Surrender: An Erotic Memoir* (2006), the narrator sites "cars, calls, bills, mortgages, food, family, schedules, money" as "subjects of controversy and control" which "destroy the erotic bond".[43] In a similar vein, Abby Lee's narrator observes how the "familiarity and repetitiveness of our daily lives can manifest itself in the way we have sex with our partners".[44]

The majority of memoirs hold such positions largely due to a widespread conviction that sexuality should not be restricted by any aspect of social obligation or social arrangement. In Catherine Townsend's *Breaking the Rules: Confessions of a Bad Girl* (2008), the narrator comments that "no matter how deviant [her] behaviour gets, doing anything near a pile of crumpled laundry can totally kill the mood",[45] and continues to declare that "women (and men) who are obsessed with appearances are far too worried about being in control to let themselves go in the sack".[46]

DOI: 10.1057/9781137326546

While these fleeting observations may appear to be unrelated, they demonstrate the narrator's belief that those who value social appearances are unable to embrace the full breadth of sexual experience. Catherine Millet's narrator presents a similar conviction: "I can no longer pretend that I really believe in God. It's quite possible that I lost this belief when I started having sexual relationships."[47] For Millet's narrator, it is difficult to reconcile the often transgressive experiences of active sexuality with higher narratives that place constraints on such expression. In the case of Millet, the limitation is imposed by a religious narrative that subjects the sexually active woman to moral condemnation, yet many other memoirs demonstrate that social limitations manifest themselves in a variety of ways and forms.

Indeed, a desire to reconceptualise sexuality as an experience that exists beyond the territory of social etiquette informs the majority of texts under discussion. In Sienna Lewis' *Intimate Adventures of an Office Girl* (2009), the narrator claims that "long-drawn-out cinematic lovemaking" is "a bit of a disadvantage when sometimes a girl just wants [...] a quick, filthy bang in the kitchen or a surprise when she bends over in the shower".[48] While this may seem nothing more than a contravention of gendered romantic scripts and the manner in which women are confined within such scripts, I would argue that Lewis is more concerned with attempting to convey – albeit in a rather clumsy and charmless manner – that sexual desire cannot be confined to any sphere of social behaviour; that sex is resistant to civilising processes. This is certainly suggested in the narrator's description of a sexual encounter with her partner: "When we lose our clothes we lose all that awkwardness and misunderstanding, and we meet on the same level of pure lust, revelling in each other's bodies."[49] Later in her memoir, Lewis concedes that her sexual compatibility with a lover depends on an agreement that sexual encounters should occupy a space beyond social norms: "I knew what I wanted – a tumble in the long grass – but I wasn't sure about him. He seemed a little uptight, not the type to abandon himself when the mood took him – he'd prefer candlelight in a bedroom to bright sunshine and a light breeze on his bum."[50] For Lewis, then, sex should be free, spontaneous and not be inhibited by social etiquettes that serve to legitimise the sexual contract.

Like Lewis, many authors appear to suggest that positive sexual encounters are an outcome of embracing the unrestricted and even risky aspects of sexuality. In Tracy Quan's *Diary of a Married Call Girl*

DOI: 10.1057/9781137326546

(2005), the prostitute-narrator decrees that "Nobody even pretends to be rational, much less consistent, about blow jobs and boyfriends", simply because "safe sex is a flawed concept if you actually like anything about sex."[51] For Quan, the practice of attempting to limit the risk involved in sexual encounters is counterproductive to the sexual contract and damaging to the erotic bond fostered between two parties. Many memoirs share a similar sentiment, and even promote the notion that attempts to limit and constrain sexual behaviour are impossible to implement, paralleling a common attitude towards male sexuality succinctly conveyed by Toni Bentley: "most men, when hard, don't act as if their penis is their own, but as if they have suddenly become subject to some kind of erectile radar device that forces them to relinquish all responsibility for its erratic behavior".[52] Bentley perpetuates traditional notions of male virility – and the implication that women serve as moral custodians of male sexual behaviour – yet other memoirs construct women's sexuality as equally uncontainable.

In *Diary of a Married Call Girl*, Quan's narrator reflects, "Sometimes, though your head is thinking that the man you're in bed with is a bit of a fool, your pussy seems to smile back at him with a mind and will of its own",[53] while her debut memoir bears witness to a similar confession: "My nipples are a little too independent. They can't be told what to do and they don't want to hide. The pleasures of my pussy are more discreet: They can be obscured by my outer lips. But I can't tame the visual evidence of a tingling nipple."[54] Quan depicts, in both of her mass-market memoirs, forceful expressions of sexual desire that are ultimately benign and rewarding, yet in the literary tradition it is the sheer force of both male and female sexuality that renders it a monstrous entity. In Almudena Grandes' *The Ages of Lulu* (1993), the narrator passively watches as her "sex started to swell, to grow spectacularly, and force [her], stupidly, to be alone with it, so [she] could fully experience its grotesque metamorphosis".[55] For Grandes' narrator, sexual desire is dangerous as it generates feelings that extend beyond sexual pleasure: "My sex was becoming enlarged with something other than pleasure, nothing like the easy pleasure, the old domestic pleasure, this was nothing like that, but rather a new, annoying, irritating, even unbearable sensation, but which I couldn't do without."[56]

It is perhaps due to this particular construction of sex – as an uncontrollable entity that cannot be constrained by either self or society – that many memoirs depict sexual expression as occupying a transgressive

DOI: 10.1057/9781137326546

space. In Bentley's *The Surrender*, the narrator notes that in terms of heterosexual anal sex practices, "both male and female atheists are the most
likely backdoor enthusiasts" as it occasions "pleasure, perversion, and
possibly their only chance for the religious experience of submission".[57]
By identifying atheists as the most enthusiastic of anal-sex practitioners,
Bentley situates, like Millet, religious narratives as forces that serve to
constrain the "perversity" of sexual desires, and continues to comment
that practicing Catholics, like herself, are more likely to perform anal
sex as "merely birth control".[58] For Bentley, both her religious conviction
as a Catholic and her political conviction as a feminist place anal sex
in a transgressive space; an act that, if performed, should be for purely
pragmatic purposes such as birth control. Yet, it is precisely this climate
of religious and political prohibition that ensures that Bentley's experience of anal sex is all the more cathartic. The narrator comments that
while vaginal sex is "no longer naughty, no longer the place for defiance,
rebellion, or rebirth", anal sex is "the playground for anarchists, icono-
clasts, artists, explorers, little boys, horny men, and women desperate to
relinquish, even temporarily, the power that has been so hard won and
cruelly awarded by the feminist movement".[59]

In Suzanne Portnoy's *The Not So Invisible Woman* (2008), the narrator expresses a similar sentiment: "Fucking me up the ass was a sure-
fire way to make me come, especially if I used a bullet vibrator on my
clit at the same time. It's the combo of the forbidden and the clitoral
stimulation that pushes my buttons."[60] Similarly in a scene in which the
prostitute-narrator embraces her husband shortly after fucking another
man, Quan's memoir similarly enacts a valorisation of the forbidden:
"*He's wearing the tie that I gave him the other day, purchased with my illicit
earnings. I could feel my nipples responding as I pressed my bare skin
against a crisp cotton shirt, a silk tie.*"[61] For both Quan and Portnoy,
sexual arousal is activated by the transgression of social norms, and both
mass-market and literary memoirs depict sexual desire as thriving on
subverting notions of social and public decency. This is most apparent
in Dawn Porter's *Diaries of an Internet Lover* (2006), where the narrator
discloses the reasons behind her desire to meet strangers online and
in real life: "Exchanging emails with a total stranger then arranging to
meet them off the back of some tempting words was an adventure in
itself. Every date I went on gave me an adrenalin buzz that isn't quite the
same as when I've just gone to the pub, got off my tits, eyed someone up,
snogged their face off for a few hours."[62] Porter's sexual desire thrives in

DOI: 10.1057/9781137326546

social situations that subvert notions of private intimacy, whether meeting strangers online or "masturbating on [a plinth] outside the Anglican Cathedral in Liverpool while heavily under the influence of LSD".[63]

Porter's narrator must be understood in the context of Angela McRobbie's definition of the "phallic girl", who "gives the impression of having won equality with men by becoming like her male counterparts" by performing sex for the purposes of "light-hearted pleasure, recreational activity, hedonism, sport, reward and status". For McRobbie, this hyper masculinised sexuality can be performed by the phallic girl "without relinquishing her own desirability to men, indeed for whom such seeming masculinity enhances her desirability since she shows herself to have a similar sexual appetite to her male counterparts".[64] What is perhaps most interesting is that while McRobbie identifies the figure of the phallic girl as epitomised in popular culture by the glamour model, for her "ordinary counterpart", the girl on the street, "assuming phallicism more often simply means drinking to excess, getting into fights, throwing up in public places, swearing and being abusive, wearing very short skirts, high heels, and skimpy tops, having casual sex, often passing out on the street and having to be taken home by friends or by the police".[65] Read in this context, assuming phallicism is clearly one of the easiest, though not the most successful, ways to reject the impositions of conventional femininity. For the phallic girl, the transgression of social and public decency is positioned as inherently pleasurable for a variety of reasons, some of which are political as such acts inevitably transgress notions of conventional femininity.

As Grandes' narrator demonstrates: "I was in a car, in the middle of the road, sucking the cock of an old friend of the family, and I felt waves of intense pleasure. I pictured myself, a fallen woman. It was wonderful."[66] The phallic girl is represented as equally adventurous as her male counterpart, and the narrator of Jenny Angell's *Callgirl* (2007) reveals that she enjoys encounters "in places that would later bring a secret sexual *frisson* – the table in the boardroom, the desk in the front of the lecture-hall, the examining-table in the doctor's office".[67] The male and female characters in popular women's memoirs occupy the same hedonistic space, both deriving pleasure from acts that subvert public decency: "His favorite moment, I think, was riding the glass elevator with me in handcuffs, potentially visible to anyone who cared to look. It certainly provoked a physical reaction. Once, he actually did come in his pants, just riding that elevator."[68] While these examples demonstrate

DOI: 10.1057/9781137326546

that, regardless of gender, individuals commonly enjoy public sex, they do not help us to understand why the authors of these memoirs stress the pleasures of public sex so extensively. To do so, it is expedient to turn our attention to Sienna Lewis' *Intimate Adventures of an Office Girl*.

Lewis' memoir, as the title suggests, is informed by a desire to defamiliarise the sexual sensibilities of the reader by convening the erotic and the habitual. The narrator positions herself as the embodiment of a pornographic dual fantasy, occupying the diametrically opposed active/passive sexual roles of "nymphomaniac" and "girl next door": "I don't want to give too much away about my everyday life so I can be as honest as possible in this blog, but I could be the receptionist in your building, the person bidding against you on an account, or the girl next to you on the bus reading her stars in *Metro*."[69] The reader's investment in the normality of the character enhances her erotic appeal, for therein resides the implication that all "normal" women have the capacity to be "nymphomaniacs" and all "normal", mundane everyday experiences can, potentially, be colonised and transformed by the erotic at any given moment. Lewis' narrator spends an enormous amount of energy demonstrating this, from admitting that she "had a wank on the office sofa, and then answered the phone without washing [her] hands",[70] to relaying accounts of public indecency: "He had a thing for running his hands across my body in public, me in my most expensive evening dress and him stroking my nipples or crotch, making me feel cheap, embarrassed and deeply, masochistically horny."[71] The narrator's shame and arousal allows the reader to identify with her as a "normal" girl who is aware of her contravention of gender and social norms, but also as a "nymphomaniac" who experiences pleasure nonetheless. In fact, in her documentation of multiple sexual encounters, Lewis' narrator often finds it necessary to express a "curious mix of mortal embarrassment and wicked excitement".[72]

What the emotional responses of Lewis' narrator reveal is, perhaps, that transgressions of public decency – and gender conventions within these contexts – are invariably pleasurable as they elicit and provoke a set of contradictory desires: to both affirm and disavow public attitudes to sexuality that attempt to restrict sexual activity to the private sphere of shame and silence. Read in this way, the transgression of social conventions, and the role this plays in precipitating sexual arousal, can be better understood by turning to the form and function of pornographic mediums. Mariana Valverde has observed how pornography sees its role

DOI: 10.1057/9781137326546

as demolishing all social barriers "by connecting, through sex, people who are generally kept separate by society's rules", arguing that the "undermining of social distinctions by the power of passion [...] is the main ingredient of erotic literature of any kind", thus validating sex as "the great leveller which eliminates all social conventions".[73] A number of popular women's memoirs demonstrate this movement – between affirming and repudiating social convention – in a number of ways. In Townsend's memoir, the narrator admits that underneath her lover's "straitlaced banker exterior lurks a serious party animal and sexual deviant, which is one of the many reasons why I adore him",[74] while Portnoy's narrator concedes: "I rather fancied a man with a posh accent talking dirty to me: the contrast between highbrow and low, posh and filth was horny."[75]

Abby Lee's memoir locates this contradiction and conflict in the context of fashion and attire, stating: "When I see a man dressed in a suit, it makes me want to rip his jacket off, pull him roughly towards me by the tie with one hand, while whipping down this zipper and freeing his cock with the other. To have him – and his suit – at my beck and call, a reversal of the power that this uniform seems to epitomise, is tantalising to me."[76] While this may appear to be driven by a desire to subvert gender convention, it is important to recognise the narrator's own awareness that a business suit is "intrinsically conservative", and represents "the suit of all capitalist moneymen and bullshit politicians". What the narrator finds so arousing is, arguably, not the suit as an embodiment of male authority, but rather the manner in which the erotic destabilises the social order that the suit represents, the "contact between the two: the cut, rigidity and conformity of the clothing juxtaposed with the hidden texture of a man's body hair, his muscular curves and the hardness of his cock".[77] As Townsend also makes clear, the attraction towards men in suits lies in the desire to release the erotic from the bonds of social proprietary: "I'm much more drawn to buttoned-up guys and revel in helping them find their wilder side."[78]

The evidence selected from a number of popular women's memoirs demonstrates that the transgression of social and public decency is positioned as pleasurable for a variety of reasons. Sexual transgression is configured as pleasurable as it affords a form of liberation against notions of normative femininity, while pleasure also derives from the provocation of contradictory emotional impulses: to both affirm and challenge conventional attitudes to sexuality. This chapter has, so far,

DOI: 10.1057/9781137326546

examined how these impulses are manifested through the integration of the erotic and the mundane in everyday contexts. Yet, it is important to consider how popular women's memoirs aggressively attempt to normalise and destigmatise "taboo" forms of sexuality that are conventionally positioned as far removed from the everyday sexual experiences of the majority.

Taboo sexuality

Commenting on the "peculiarly intimate relationship" between morality and sexual behaviour, Jeffrey Weeks states that the term "immorality" in the English language "almost invariably means sexual misbehaviour", while "moral" to a lesser but still potent extent, "implies adherence to certain agreed norms of behaviour, and types of activity".[79] Thus, immoral and moral sexual behaviour can be gauged not by the extent to which a sexual act is harmful to either self or society, but by the extent to which the sexual act deviates from what is perceived to be common sexual practice. Furthermore, what any society deems to be normative depends on the extent to which a sexual act deviates from the socially and religiously sanctioned procreational purposes of sex. Sexual activity between heterosexual married couples – the most validated form of sexual contact – is closely linked to the reproductive function of sex, while gay sex remains taboo because – among other reasons – it entirely repudiates intercourse as procreational. Returning to Gayle Rubin's conceptualisation of the erotic pyramid, this is precisely why "marital, reproductive heterosexuals are alone at the top of the erotic pyramid" while "bar dykes and promiscuous gay men" reside slightly above deviant groups at the bottom, namely "transsexuals, transvestites, fetishists, sadomasochists, sex workers such as prostitutes and porn models, and the lowliest of all, those whose eroticism transgresses generational boundaries".[80]

While it is difficult to deny Rubin's appraisal, it also important to bear in mind that sexuality remains a difficult issue to negotiate even in the context of heterosexual relationships. The association of sex with shame can afflict any individual regardless of their sexual orientation and marital status. Shame is an emotional response that rests on the assumption that male and female sexual organs are an "intrinsically inferior part of the body, much lower and less holy than the mind".[81] Even though Rubin

DOI: 10.1057/9781137326546

comments that "solitary sex floats ambiguously",[82] neither at the top nor bottom of her erotic pyramid, many popular memoirs demonstrate that masturbation remains, even in the 21st century, taboo for many women and yet another source of sexual anxiety. Sienna Lewis' narrator recalls her childhood discovery of self-pleasure: "'How do you manage to touch yourself?' I asked another friend, Judy, disgusted by the thought of putting my bare hand 'there'. She told me she used rubber gloves, and gave me a pair she'd nicked from her parents' medicine cupboard."[83] Lewis' recollection confirms that the association of sex with shame is part of a socialisation process in which girls learn the interdependency of sexual feelings, romantic love and moral precepts. This value extends from childhood to adulthood, and across many contemporary memoirs, thus when Krissy Kneen's narrator transgresses the sexual codes of society, we bear witness not only to expressions of guilt, but also anxieties regarding her close proximity to stereotypes of sexual transgression: "I wasn't the type of lady who accompanied a gentleman home upon first meeting. This wasn't a bend in the rule – it was a snap. This behavior was reserved for girls with daddy issues, plagued with low self-esteem, for women who wore leather hotpants."[84]

Acutely aware of the moral and ideological pressures that accompany sexual activity beyond monogamy, many of the memoirs discussed in this book actively engage in a process of normalising notionally subversive female sexual action. In Dawn Porter's *Diaries of an Internet Lover*, the narrator declares "I'm not ashamed to say that I love sex for all that it is",[85] while Suzanne Portnoy's narrator confesses to feeling "like a sex therapist" when reassuring a lover that "bodily fluids exist and are natural".[86] These particular memoirs aim to normalise female heterosexual promiscuity, yet others, perhaps more significantly, function as vehicles that encourage the popular fiction reader to rebuke the perceived interdependency of taboo sexuality and immorality. In Tracy Quan's *Diary of a Manhattan Call Girl*, the narrator challenges negative attitudes to sex work and sex workers. She achieves this by challenging the commonly held perception of sex workers as chaotic and unstable, declaring that her parents would "fear for [her] safety, for the security of [her] possessions and [her] body" if they were aware of her true vocation, assuming that "a hooker is someone whose household can be turned upside down at any moment".[87] Antithetical to this stereotype, Quan's narrator is eloquent and educated, yet it is "completely outside" the "placid middle-class lifestyle"[88] of her parents to envision a girl like their daughter working as a social escort.

DOI: 10.1057/9781137326546

The narrator of Miss S.' *Confessions of a Working Girl* (2007) conveys a similar gap between reality and perception: "The scary feeling of who knows what and the worry that they are going to use the knowledge against you is the hardest thing about this kind of work. The misconceptions, the shame, being judged because of what you do."[89]

The narrator continues to claim that stigmas surrounding sex work are generated by avenues of misinformation that construct the popular image of the prostitute as depraved, contaminated and abject. Miss S. declares that "the image of the filthy, diseased whore" always "makes [her] laugh" because prostitutes are "technically one of the sexually safest demographic groups in the country".[90] Emerging from this position of stigmatisation, many popular women's memoirs aim to recalibrate sex work as a vocation in which individuals should be accorded dignity and equity. Miss S. achieves this by presenting herself as a sex worker in control, and sex work as a pragmatic and carefully considered choice:

> The whole thing felt secure, in general. At least I wasn't getting blind drunk like the rest of the student girls in the dorms and going off with strangers, waking up in strange places, not knowing where they were or how they got there! [...] The irony is that me and my fellow girls get tarred with the cheap-slut/whore brush while there are people out there who do it for free and take huge risks.[91]

By circumnavigating the risks, both physical and social, of promiscuity without financial remuneration, Miss S.' narrator rejects the conceptualisation of the sex worker as chaotic and pathological. Quan's narrator demonstrates the same concerns and is fearful of being associated with the deviant image of the sex worker, and for this reason avoids letting clients know she is married:

> What if they think I married a guy who can't support me or mistreats me, that I turn tricks in order to make ends meet? Maybe they'll think I have to support *him*? I don't want my customers to think I'm that kind of hooker [...] If you seem to be the kind of call girl who marries a ne'er-do-well or behaves foolishly with men, the clients lose respect.[92]

The fact that Quan's narrator is even concerned with her client's perception of her demonstrates the extent to which contemporary women's memoirs aim to reconfigure taboo sexual practices as socially legitimate. In Quan's memoir, it is the notion of "prostitute professionalism" that validates commercial sexual activity as neither immoral nor low-class. Quan mobilises this message through constructing characters who are

DOI: 10.1057/9781137326546

not only sex workers, but also feminists actively engaged in destigmatising and politicising their occupation. The memoir features Roxana Blair, founder of the New York Council of Trollops (NYCOT), and Allie, an enthusiastic debutante in the world of sex-work activism. Allie's contribution to NYCOT is manifested through her Internet literacy and dynamism, a woman with "a mouse pad that proclaimed SAFE SEX SLUT in white block letters"[93] and whose Internet savvy ensures global networking with sex workers in Thailand:

> Against a pistachio-colored background, a series of magenta greetings – Hola ... *Bonjour* ... *Sawadee Kha* – wiggled slowly across the screen. When Allie clicked on the dollar sign, hot pink condoms tumbled forth, followed by a montage of dancing girls with long black hair and light brown skin in bikinis and heels: ENTERTAINMENT WORKERS SANS FRONTIERES.[94]

Through Allie's global networking, NYCOT collaborate with *Bad Girls Without Borders* – a Thai feminist organisation that aims to protect the rights of sex workers – and the relationship culminates in Noi, the organisation's Bangkok coordinator, becoming a keynote speaker at a "Colloquial on Informal Economies" at an Ivy League school. While this is, of course, an absurd narrative turn, what is perhaps more important is Quan's desire to politicise sex work and, through the popular memoir, create a utopian landscape in which taboo female sexuality is removed from the margins for the popular audience. As the most conspicuously fictionalised memoir discussed in this book, Quan's is able to exert greater flexibility in conveying its political intent.

While prostitution remains a theme commonly explored in popular women's memoirs, many of the texts discussed in this book also interrogate more extreme forms of taboo sexuality, and pay particular attention to paedophilia and childhood sexuality. At the beginning of Almudena Grandes' *The Ages of Lulu*, where the narrator tastes semen for the first time, the author makes a conceptual link between sexual activity and childhood experience: "a hot, viscous substance, both sweet and sour, with a slight aftertaste like medicines which ruined many a happy childhood".[95] The simile operates as a narrative precursor, preparing the reader for later events in which Grandes explores, only to subvert, a conventional theme: the relationship between predatory male sexuality and childhood innocence. In Grandes' memoir the 15-year-old narrator, Lulu, begins a sexual relationship with Pablo, an older man who describes her pubic hair as a monstrous obscenity: "Because you're very dark; you're too hairy for a fifteen-year-old. You don't have a little girl's cunt. And I like little girls with little girls' cunts, especially when I'm about to debauch them".[96] Paralleling this theme, Miss S.' *Confessions of a Working Girl* draws attention to a prostitute's experience with male clients who require her to perform childhood femininity: "My least favourite ones, and I had quite a lot, liked me because I looked like a little girl, and they would bounce me on their knee and get me to call them daddy or teacher."[97] While this negative reaction to the demands of her clients is entirely understandable, what is most striking is that Miss S.' memoir is, in this respect, an anomaly among the texts surveyed in this book. In fact, most popular memoirs serve to radically subvert both the notion that children are sexually passive, and the notion that adult–child sexual relationships are exploitative and damaging.

Indeed, for while Grandes appears to initially position Pablo as a predatory paedophile, the reader quickly learns that Lulu embraces the relationship: "Somewhere inside my head, far back enough so it didn't bother me, but near enough to be noticeable, throbbed the fact that I was under-age, six years to go before I was twenty-one."[98] Grandes locates Lulu's desire for Pablo as outcome of a latent father–daughter sexual relationship, for even though the narrator does not have sex with her father, she concedes "I understood that he desired me, even though he was my father, and I desired him, terribly."[99] Pablo becomes, therefore, an eroticised surrogate father, and Lulu's real father remains an object of sexual fantasy: "I'd take his hand and pull it towards me until it touched my sex. I'd choose one of his fingers and rub it against me. 'I'm a big girl now, I need it, Daddy'."[100] Like many of the memoirs discussed in this book, Grandes' does not construct literal sexual relationships between fathers and daughters, and the familial sexual relationship remains preserved as a taboo space. Yet, by accentuating father–daughter sexual desire in the context of not only imaginative fantasy, but also in literal cross-generational relationships, Grandes positions the father–daughter dynamic as a mirror image of the power dynamic within which male/female heterosexual relationships operate. As fathers represent, to their daughters, figures of consummate male authority, and as male power is eroticised in all patriarchal societies, it is perhaps hardly surprising that the father/daughter relationship is so frequently an opportunity for erotic exploration.

This may explain why, in Toni Bentley's *The Surrender*, anal sex is positioned as a recuperation of an affirmative father–daughter relationship:

DOI: 10.1057/9781137326546

"Being sodomized now, by choice, reconciles this injury with a scenario of the dominant male and the obedient little girl. Instead of rejection and criticism, I am told, 'Good girl, good girl.' The nastier I am and the better I suck his cock, the better I am, until I'm the goodest little girl in the world."[101] The "injury" that Bentley refers to is her difficult relationship with her father during childhood, and the sexual relationship is positioned as a nostalgic recuperation of vanquished father–daughter bonds. In this context, the transgressive behaviour of the "daughter" is not punished but rewarded ("the nastier I am and the better I suck his cock, the better I am"), reclaiming a traumatic childhood experience as positive and the father–daughter relationship as harmonious. The memoirs of Grandes and Bentley validate, in different ways, sexual experience as a way of recovering problematic father–daughter relationships, and appear to assert that childhood sexuality is both active and affirmative, both literally and imaginatively. Similar to the manner in which contemporary erotic memoirs reposition other forms of taboo sexuality, notably sex work, as not necessarily constituted by only negative experiences, Grandes and Bentley focus on the manner in which childhood sexuality, even in paedophilic relationships, is positively experienced and shapes erotic activity in adult life.

Tracy Quan's *Diary of a Manhattan Call Girl* offers the most contentious representation of childhood sexuality by subverting attitudes to sex work and paedophilia simultaneously. Quan's narrator, Nancy Chan, declares that "ever since the age of ten, [she] wanted to be a hooker – and before that, a *Playboy* centrefold",[102] and later the memoir presents the impact of pornography on her developing sexuality:

> At eleven, I discovered a porno paperback called *Little Girls for Sale* in the back of a poster shop that also sold used books. On the cover was an illustration of a doll-faced child with big round eyes wearing a babyish dress. She looked about eight. But the girls in the story were twelve and fourteen – not little girls at all, I remember thinking. The imaginary and rather infantile cover child was a hoax. Nobody over the age of nine dressed like that! As one who was no longer a "little" girl, I had a stake in these issues. But the title itself gave me hope [...] The not-so-little girls were temptresses, instigators. They had secret sexual encounters in public places. A man in a supermarket was lured by a twelve-year-old girl who made her small breasts available to him by leaning over the frozen food section. He touched her tentatively, while nobody was looking. But before all this happened, she had bewitched him in the soap aisle. He had followed her all over the store.[103]

DOI: 10.1057/9781137326546

It is not surprising that, as an 11-year-old, Chan refuses to perceive the slightly older adolescents as "little girls", but what is surprising is the level of sexual desire generated in the narrator by the sexually active child protagonists of the text: "As I flipped through the book, my body surprised and embarrassed me. I was standing in the back of the poster shop, quietly aroused, but it was totally unexpected. I swelled up, my whole body seemed to be more alive, my face felt flushed, and my heart was beating faster."[104] While *Little Girls for Sale* was presumably produced for the pleasure of an adult male audience, Chan's tactile response to the text offers another interesting reconfiguration of childhood sexuality as actively experienced.

While it could be feasibly argued that Chan's young narrator is merely erotising the conditions of her oppression by demonstrating a sexuality activated by male pornographic scripts, she nevertheless reveals that her childhood decision to enter prostitution was, in fact, politically motivated: "When I decided, at ten, that I wanted to be a prostitute, I had never even heard of an orgasm. I knew that I wanted sex to be my career, the source of my independence, what I spent my days doing – when I grew up."[105] After entering prostitution, the child sex worker is ostensibly an innocent ("I was almost fifteen. It never occurred to me that being underage was something I could charge more for, so I told him I was nineteen"),[106] yet the narrative enacts a complete reversal of the conventional "paedophile-as-predator" and "child-as-victim" paradigm. After meeting a known local paedophile, Professor Andrews, Chan comments "I doubt that he'd ever had a Sexual Plan when he was my age. And where I was too clinical to know what passion was, he was unable to control the urges that were most dangerous to his reputation."[107] In the text, it is the adult male's decadent and uncontrollable sexuality that is exploited by a child-prostitute in complete control of her sexual life: "Professor Andrews was part of a summer project I had assigned myself just before the break: I was determined to start taking the Pill, to start having a Sex Life."[108] After seducing Andrews, but refusing to perform sexual pleasure in the encounter, Chan proudly declares, "It's horrible, really, when you think about it – how cold a pubescent girl can be in the face of a pedophile's lechery."[109] Quan's narrator appears empowered, yet like all of the memoirs discussed in this book, it is impossible to determine if this is merely a form of postfeminist posturing; attempting a façade of agency and sexual knowingness by self-identifying as an aspiring phallic

DOI: 10.1057/9781137326546

girl, even in childhood. After all, if the postfeminist masquerade erroneously endows women with agency, this is perhaps even truer of popular
culture's construction of contemporary girlhood, in which neo-liberal
pronouncements of personal choice negate any positioning of girls as
victims.

This chapter has aimed to explore how popular women's memoirs
position sexual desire as constitutionally transgressive, situating sexual
passion as a necessarily violent force that functions to subvert social
norms and institutional values. The chapter has focused on the manner in which the memoirs serve to destigmatise and normalise taboo
sexual identities and behaviours commonly perceived to be deviant,
challenging the notion that sadomasochism is based on patriarchal
power structures, that female childhood sexuality is dormant, and
that cross-generational/paedophilic sexual relationships are always
exploitative. The memoirs have demonstrated that subversions of public
decency – and gender conventions within these contexts – are invariably pleasurable as they elicit and provoke a set of contradictory desires:
to both affirm and disavow public attitudes to sexuality that attempt
to restrict sexual activity to the private sphere of shame and silence.
Popular erotic memoirs examine these contradictory impulses through
the integration of the erotic and the mundane in everyday locales, and
especially in their attempts to normalise and destigmatise taboo forms
of sexuality that are conventionally positioned as far removed from the
everyday sexual experiences of the majority. What remains difficult
to resolve, however, especially for the feminist critic, is the extent to
which these gender subversions are really subversive at all, or even
empowering. While it is clear that popular women's memoirs aim to
reconfigure taboo sexual practices as socially legitimate, especially via
their propagation of the notion that women do not always embrace the
healthy and wholesome aspects of human experience, it is impossible to
determine the extent to which these feminine subjectivities are authentic indicators of pleasure, especially in memoirs such as Quan's where
the fictionalized elements are all too apparent. And most importantly of
all, while all of the women in the memoirs discussed in this book appear
to express sexual agency, the extent to which their sexual desires, object
choices and sexual motivations accord so harmoniously with those of
their male counterparts may leave the reader feeling highly suspicious
of any claim to agency.

DOI: 10.1057/9781137326546

Notes

1 Michael Warner, *The Trouble with Normal: Sex, Politics and the Ethics of Queer Life* (Cambridge, MA: Harvard University Press, 2000 [1999]), 2.
2 Warner, *The Trouble with Normal*, 2.
3 Gayle Rubin, "Thinking Sex: Notes for a Radical Theory of the Politics of Sexuality" in *Pleasure and Danger: Exploring Female Sexuality*, ed. Carol Vance (London: Pandora Press, 1989), 278.
4 Ibid., 279.
5 Ibid.
6 Jeffrey Weeks, *Sexuality* (London and New York: Routledge, 2003), 112.
7 Carol Vance, "Pleasure and Danger: Towards a Politics of Sexuality" in *Pleasure and Danger: Exploring Female Sexuality*, ed. Carol Vance (London: Pandora Press, 1989), 3.
8 Clarissa Smith, "Pleasing Intensities: Masochism and Affective Pleasure in Porn Short Fictions" in *Mainstreaming Sex: The Sexualization of Western Culture*, ed. Fiona Attwood (London: I.B. Tauris, 2009), 30.
9 Andrea Dworkin, *Letters from a War Zone: Writings 1976–1987* (London: Secker and Warburg, 1988), 264.
10 Robert Jensen, *Getting Off: Pornography and the End of Masculinity* (Cambridge, MA: South End Press, 2007), 75.
11 Gail Dines, *Pornland: How Porn Has Hijacked Our Sexuality* (Boston, MA: Beacon Press, 2010), 96.
12 Becky McLaughlin, "Sex Cuts" in *Jane Sexes It Up: True Confessions of Feminist Desire*, ed. Merri Lisa Johnson (New York: Four Walls, Eight Windows, 2002), 82.
13 Chris Daley, "Of the Flesh Fancy: Spanking and the Single Girl" in *Jane Sexes It Up: True Confessions of Feminist Desire*, ed. Merri Lisa Johnson (New York: Four Walls Eight Windows, 2002), 130.
14 Naomi Wolf, *Promiscuities: A Secret History of Female Desire* (London: Vintage, 1998), 170.
15 Lynne Segal, *Is the Future Female?: Troubled Thoughts on Contemporary Feminism* (London: Virago, 1987), 99.
16 Ibid.
17 Catherine Millet, *The Sexual Life of Catherine M.*, trans. Adriana Hunter (London: Corgi Books, 2003 [2002]), 67.
18 Ibid., 100.
19 Smith, "Pleasing Intensities", 33.
20 Linda Williams, *Hard Core: Power, Pleasure and the "Frenzy of the Visible"* (London: Pandora Press, 1991), 196.
21 Ibid.

DOI: 10.1057/9781137326546

22 Merri Lisa Johnson, "Fuck You and Your Untouchable Face: Third Wave Feminism and the Problem of Romance" in *Jane Sexes It Up: True Confessions of Feminist Desire*, ed. Merri Lisa Johnson (New York: Four Walls Eight Windows, 2002), 42.

23 Ibid., 43.

24 Melissa P., *One Hundred Strokes of the Brush before Bed*, trans. Lawrence Venuti (London: Serpent's Tail, 2004), 2.

25 Krissy Kneen, *Affection: An Erotic Memoir* (Berkeley, California: Seal Press, 2010), 72.

26 Ibid., 84.

27 Suzanne Portnoy, *The Not So Invisible Woman* (London: Virgin Books, 2008), 7.

28 Belle de Jour, *The Intimate Adventures of a London Call Girl* (London: Phoenix, 2005), 2.

29 Warner, *The Trouble with Normal*, 5.

30 Melissa P., *One Hundred Strokes*, 31.

31 Ibid., 93.

32 Almudena Grandes, *The Ages of Lulu*, trans. S. Soto (London: Phoenix, 2005 [1993]), 149.

33 Ibid., 134.

34 Millet, *The Sexual Life of Catherine M.*, 23.

35 Daley, "Of the Flesh Fancy", 131.

36 Williams, *Hard Core*, 195.

37 de Jour , *The Intimate Adventures of a London Call Girl*, 55.

38 Ibid., 121.

39 Wolf, *Promiscuities: A Secret History of Female Desire*, 131.

40 Ibid., 123.

41 Ibid.

42 Kneen, *Affection: An Erotic Memoir*, 176.

43 Toni Bentley, *The Surrender: An Erotic Memoir* (London: Harper Perennial, 2006), 31.

44 Abby Lee, *Girl with a One Track Mind: Confessions of the Seductress Next Door* (London: Ebury Press, 2006), 34.

45 Catherine Townsend, *Breaking the Rules: Confessions of a Bad Girl* (London: John Murray, 2008), 24.

46 Ibid., 113.

47 Millet, *The Sexual Life of Catherine M.*, 32.

48 Sienna Lewis, *Intimate Adventures of an Office Girl* (London: Avon Books, 2009), 18.

49 Ibid., 45.

50 Ibid., 12.

51 Tracy Quan, *Diary of a Married Call Girl* (London: Harper Perennial, 2006 [2005]), 232.

DOI: 10.1057/9781137326546

52 Bentley, *The Surrender*, 125.
53 Quan, *Diary of a Married Call Girl*, 208.
54 Tracy Quan, *Diary of a Manhattan Call Girl* (London: Harper Perennial, 2005 [2001]), 40.
55 Almudena Grandes, *The Ages of Lulu*, trans. Sonia Soto (London: Phoenix, 2005 [1993]), 47.
56 Ibid., 19.
57 Bentley, *The Surrender*, 114.
58 Ibid.
59 Ibid., 84.
60 Portnoy, *The Not So Invisible Woman*, 107.
61 Quan, *Diary of a Married Call Girl*, 40 (emphasis in the original).
62 Dawn Porter, *Diaries of an Internet Lover* (London: Virgin Books, 2006), 4.
63 Ibid., 24.
64 Angela McRobbie, *The Aftermath of Feminism: Gender, Culture and Social Change* (London: Sage, 2009), 83.
65 Ibid., 84.
66 Grandes, *The Ages of Lulu*, 23.
67 Jenny Angell, *Callgirl* (London: Avon, 2007), 109.
68 Ibid., 305.
69 Lewis, *Intimate Adventures of an Office Girl*, 5.
70 Ibid., 49.
71 Ibid., 127.
72 Ibid., 160.
73 Mariana Valverde, "Pornography: Not For Men Only" in *Sexual Lives: A Reader on the Theories and Realities of Human Sexualities*, eds Betsy Crane and Robert Heasley (New York: McGraw-Hill, 2003), 471.
74 Townsend, *Breaking the Rules*, 2.
75 Suzanne Portnoy, *The Butcher, the Baker, the Candlestick Maker* (London: Virgin Books, 2006), 68.
76 Lee, *Girl with a One Track Mind*, 167.
77 Ibid., 166.
78 Townsend, *Breaking the Rules*, 69.
79 Jeffrey Weeks, *Invented Moralities: Sexual Values in an Age of Uncertainty* (New York: Columbia University Press, 1995), 46.
80 Rubin, "Thinking Sex: Notes for a Radical Theory of the Politics of Sexuality", 279.
81 Ibid., 278.
82 Ibid., 279.
83 Lewis, *Intimate Adventures of an Office Girl*, 3.
84 Klein, *Affection*, 24.
85 Porter, *Diaries of an Internet Lover*, 2.

DOI: 10.1057/9781137326546

86   Portnoy, *The Butcher*, 15.
87   Quan, *Diary of a Manhattan Call Girl*, 185–186.
88   Ibid.
89   Miss S., *Confessions of a Working Girl* (London: Penguin Books, 2007), 221.
90   Ibid.
91   Ibid., 89.
92   Quan, *Diary of a Married Call Girl*, 32.
93   Ibid., 66.
94   Ibid.
95   Grandes, *The Ages of Lulu*, 48.
96   Ibid., 38.
97   Miss S., *Confessions of a Working Girl*, 146.
98   Grandes, *The Ages of Lulu*, 22.
99   Ibid., 112.
100   Ibid.
101   Bentley, *The Surrender*, 138.
102   Quan, *Diary of a Manhattan Call Girl*, 88.
103   Ibid., 214.
104   Ibid.
105   Ibid.
106   Ibid., 80.
107   Ibid., 77.
108   Ibid., 76.
109   Ibid.

DOI: 10.1057/9781137326546

Conclusion

Abstract: *Recognising that popular erotic memoirs represent and embody the significant changes experienced by women in Western cultures over the last 20 years, this chapter balances both the empowering and disempowering aspects of the genre, concluding that this new phenomenon in commercial publishing both celebrates and undermines women's sexual agency.*

Gwynne, Joel. *Erotic Memoirs and Postfeminism: The Politics of Pleasure.* Basingstoke: Palgrave Macmillan, 2013. DOI: 10.1057/9781137326546.

Commenting on the growth of second-wave feminism in the early 1970s, Lynne Segal makes the observation that women's groups did not identify men as a central problem in the movement towards liberation, but were more concerned with "attacking the language and iconography of a form of 'sexual liberation' in which women as 'chicks' remained the passive objects of men's desires, instead of the self-affirming subjects of their own".[1] While the 1960s marked the emergence of liberal forms of sexual ethics concomitant with more discursive forms of social activism – most notably in the US – many second-wave feminists rejected the sexually libertarian femininity of the "flower child" as a nothing more than a manifestation of men's sexual fantasies. The function of femininity in female empowerment has always been a controversial topic in feminist discourse, and no more so than in the late-20th century and into the new millennium. In accordance with postfeminism's centralisation of the "woman as pinup, the enduring linchpin of commercial beauty culture",[2] the popular media has resolutely repackaged femininity as an identity and performance that is simultaneously passive and active. Women's erotic memoirs are thoroughly invested in this paradigm, and reconfigure femininity in a number of ways. The texts discussed in this book validate mainstream models of hyperfemininity in terms of outward appearance, but also subvert femininity through the aggressive articulation of sexual desires and expectations. As contemporary popular culture has become increasingly sexualised, and as feminist critical discourse has become more tolerant to the liberating possibilities of promiscuity, pinning down and evaluating the politics of female sexual activity is an increasingly difficult endeavour. Even though it remains a challenge to position promiscuity as either specifically feminist or anti-feminist, it could be argued that such a contradictory movement – between first affirming and then disavowing conventionally feminine behaviour – forces the reader of erotic memoirs to ask a number of questions regarding the problems and possibilities of empowerment within such fragmented and contradictory terms.

The memoirs explored in this book can be positioned as empowering, in many ways. They showcase third-wave feminist sensibilities by expressing hostility towards reactionary cultures that still uphold the values of sexual essentialism. A movement towards egalitarianism between the sexes – based on mutual sexual understanding – are sentiments that bind many of the memoirs. They are also empowering in their explicit discussion of sexual activity, contesting the manner in which female

DOI: 10.1057/9781137326546

sexual expression is socially restricted and usually confined within a commercialised perception of sexual liberation that circumnavigates frank discussions of sexual preference. This is often manifested in the female colonisation of the historically male terrain of anatomical objectification, and the memoirs' emphasis on redirecting female investment to the realm of sexual intimacy, rather than emotional intimacy, accords with contemporary feminist perspectives of the limitations and constraints of heterosexual romance. The memoirs demonstrate that, in the 21st century, women taking the initiative in love and sex has become a common cultural theme, in accordance with a more expansive dissolution of the link between emotional and sexual intimacy. They resolutely document an inversion of the traditional social pattern of female sexuality activated and validated by romantic love, and position emotional intimacy as a culmination of, and dependant on, satisfactory sexual exchanges. Whether due to the endemic mainstreaming of the sex industry and the sexualisation of Western cultures, or merely a consequence of second-wave feminist thought that implicated romance narratives as detrimental to female selfhood, there is little doubt that many of the memoirs locate emotional intimacy as irrelevant to positive sexual encounters. If understood in this way, the memoirs serve to publicise and normalise female promiscuity in a world where female sexuality is subject to constraints, control and condemnation. The memoirs provide a space for contemporary women to present permanent and public testimonies of their engagement in the sexual world and abilities to perform as sexual beings. Therein certainly resides the subversive potential of these texts, especially if we bear in mind the historical suppression of female sexuality and the restriction of female desire to zones protected and privileged in cultures. Acutely aware of the moral and ideological pressures that accompany sexual activity, many of the memoirs discussed in this book are radical in their commitment to normalising notionally subversive female sexual action.

Yet, it remains difficult to entirely embrace women's erotic memoirs as liberating, positive and empowering, for the majority valorise submission to heterosexual male dominance, even when flamboyantly championing the rhetoric of the postfeminist liberated subject. While the women in these texts forcefully express their sexual desires and expectations, these desires often remain unfulfilled, and sexual encounters are frequently dominated by male desires and expectations. Sex is often experienced and described in a manner comparable to male-produced pornography,

DOI: 10.1057/9781137326546

and the memoirs fail to promote female sexual self-definition outside of pornographic paradigms by doing almost nothing to radically restructure the conventions of mass pornography. While the literary memoirs discussed in this book are politically self-reflexive – especially in their appropriation of the pornographic male gaze through an itemisation of the bodies of men – female empowerment in mass-market memoirs is often contingent upon a sexual objectification that is entirely self-willed. Yet, what is perhaps most problematic – at least from a feminist perspective – is the dominance of ostensibly abusive sexual fantasies in women's memoirs, whether imagined alone or as an appendage to real sexual encounters. In a similar vein, mass-market memoirs position acts of both material sexual violence and performative S/M as essential to positive sexual experiences as they subvert, or at least supplement, genital focused intercourse. While this can be interpreted as a form of resistance to sexual acts that centre on male penetration and penile pleasure, it raises questions regarding why these memoirs appear to always position women as the objects rather than the instigators of sex and sexual violence. The texts rarely document any form of pleasure that is not dependant on male aggression, and the reader is expected to perceive this as empowering simply because the authors/narrators claim to enjoy these experiences.

The memoirs discussed in this book demonstrate that contemporary women certainly recognise the importance of expressing their sexual selves, but they also demonstrate the inability of contemporary women to truly own their bodies. This contradictory state is distinct in the contemporary historical moment, for while postfeminism is indicative of a posttraditional era characterised by "dramatic changes in basic social relationships, role stereotyping and conceptions of agency",[3] many of these ostensibly dramatic developments are often only cosmetic modifications of reactionary gender regimes. When women express pleasure in passivity – sexual or otherwise – postfeminist empowerment can be positioned as an especially insidious conceit in its allocation of regressive roles to men and women while celebrating the latter's complicity in this allocation. This pattern of behaviour is a particularly disconcerting trend where popular erotic memoirs are concerned, as the form holds so much potential for feminist consciousness-raising. Even though scholars such as Kathy Myers have recognised the feminist potential of female-authored erotica, commenting that "questions of representation and of pleasure cannot be separated", and that "a feminist erotica could examine

DOI: 10.1057/9781137326546

the nature of this relationship",[4] one cannot avoid concluding that popular women's erotic memoirs – while framed as liberating – continue to celebrate male sexual-domination.

Notes

1 Lynne Segal, "The Belly of the Beast: Sex as Male Domination?" in *The Masculinities Reader*, eds Stephen Whitehead and Frank Barrett (London: Polity Press, 2001), 100.

2 Yvonne Tasker and Diane Negra, "Feminist Politics and Postfeminist Culture" in *Interrogating Postfeminism: Gender and the Politics of Popular Culture,* eds Diane Negra and Yvonne Tasker (Durham: Duke University Press, 2007), 3.

3 Stephanie Genz and Benjamin Brabon, *Postfeminism: Cultural Texts and Theories* (Edinburgh: Edinburgh University Press, 2009), 1.

4 Kathy Myers, "Towards a Feminist Erotica" in *Sexual Lives: A Reader on the Theories and Realities of Human Sexuality,* eds Betsy Crane and Robert Heasley (New York: McGraw-Hill, 2003), 485.

DOI: 10.1057/9781137326546

Bibliography

Angell, Jenny. *Callgirl*. London: Avon, 2007.

Attwood, Feona. *Mainstreaming Sex: The Sexualisation of Western Cultures*. London: I.B. Tauris, 2009.

Attwood, Feona (ed). *Porn.com: Making Sense of Online Pornography*. New York: Peter Lang, 2010.

Attwood, Feona. "Porn Studies: From Social Problem to Cultural Practice" in *Porn.com: Making Sense of Online Pornography*, ed. Feona Attwood (New York: Peter Lang, 2010), 1–14.

Bataille, Georges. *Eroticism*. Translated by M. Dalwood. London: Penguin, 2001 (1954).

Baumgardner, Jennifer and Amy Richards. *Manifesta: Young Women, Feminism and the Future*. New York: Farrar, Straus and Giroux, 2010 [2000].

Beasley, Chris. *Gender and Sexuality: Critical Theories, Critical Thinkers*. London: Sage, 2005.

Bentley, Toni. *The Surrender: An Erotic Memoir*. London: Harper Perennial, 2006.

Bishop, Mardia J. "The Making of a Pre-Pubescent Porn Star: Contemporary Fashion for Elementary School Girls" in *Pop-Porn: Pornography in American Culture*, eds M.J. Bishop and A.C. Hall, (Westport, CT: Praeger Publishers, 2007), 45–56.

Breton, Andre. *Manifestoes of Surrealism*. Translated by R. Seaver and H.R. Lane. Ann Arbor: University of Michigan Press, 1998 [1924].

Bristow, Joseph. *Sexuality*. London and New York: Routledge, 1997.

DOI: 10.1057/9781137326546

Brod, Harry. "Pornography and the Alimentation of Male Sexuality" in *Sexual Lives: A Reader on the Theories and Realities of Human Sexuality*, eds Betsy Crane and Robert Heasley (New York: McGraw-Hill, 2003), 477–485.

Budgeon, Shelley. "Fashion Magazine Advertising: Constructing Femininity in the 'Postfeminist' Era" in *Gender and Utopia in Advertising: A Critical Reader*, eds Luigi Manca and Alessandra Manda (Lisle, IL: Procopian Press, 1994), 60–74.

Califia, Pat. "Feminism and Sadomasochism" in *Feminism and Sexuality: A Reader*, eds Stevi Jackson and Sue Scott (Edinburgh: Edinburgh University Press, 1996), 230–237.

Cooper, Al, Irene Mcloughlin, and Kevin Campbell. "Sexuality in Cyberspace: Update for the 21st Century", *CyberPsychology and Behaviour 3*, vol. 4 (2000): 520–543.

Coward, Rosalind. "Sex after Aids" in *Feminism and Sexuality: A Reader*, eds Stevi Jackson and Sue Scott (Edinburgh: Edinburgh University Press, 1996), 245–247.

Daley, Chris. "Of the Flesh Fancy: Spanking and the Single Girl" in *Jane Sexes It Up: True Confessions of Feminist Desire*, ed. Merri Lisa Johnson (New York: Four Walls Eight Windows, 2002), 127–138.

de Jour, Belle. *Intimate Adventures of a London Call Girl*. London: Phoenix, 2005.

Dines, Gail. *Pornland: How Porn Has Hijacked Our Sexuality*. Boston, MA: Beacon Press, 2010.

Dworkin, Andrea. *Letters from a War Zone: Writings 1976–1987*. London: Secker and Warburg, 1988.

Freud, Sigmund. "The Sexual Aberrations" in *Three Essays on the Theory of Sexuality*. Translated by James Strachey (New York: Basic Books, 1987), 18–29.

Gamble, Sarah. "Postfeminism" in *The Routledge Companion to Feminism and Postfeminism*, ed. Sarah Gamble (London and New York: Routledge, 1998), 43–51.

Genz, Stephanie and Benjamin Brabon. *Postfeminism: Cultural Texts and Theories*. Edinburgh: Edinburgh University Press, 2009.

Giddens, Anthony. *The Transformation of Intimacy: Sexuality, Love and Eroticism in Modern Societies*. Cambridge: Polity Press, 1992.

Gill, Rosalind. *Gender and the Media*. Cambridge: Polity Press, 2006.

Glitre, Kathrina. "Nancy Meyers and Popular Feminism" in *Women on Screen: Feminism and Femininity in Visual Culture*, ed. Melanie Waters (Basingstoke: Palgrave Macmillan, 2011), 17–30.

DOI: 10.1057/9781137326546

Grandes, Almudena. *The Ages of Lulu*. Translated by Sonia Soto. London: Phoenix, 2005 [1993].

Hardy, Simon. "The New Pornographies: Representation or Reality?" in *Mainstreaming Sex: The Sexualization of Western Cultures*, ed. Feona Attwood (London: I.B. Tauris, 2009), 8–19.

Hite, Shere. *The Hite Report on the Family: Growing Up under Patriarchy*. London: Bloomsbury, 1994.

Holland, Janet, Carol Ramazanoglu, Sue Sharpe and Rachel Thomson. "Pressured Pleasure: Young Women and the Negotiation of Sexual Boundaries" in *Feminism and Sexuality: A Reader*, eds Stevie Jackson and Sue Scott (Edinburgh: Edinburgh University Press, 1996), 248–262.

Jackson, Stevi. "Heterosexuality, Power and Pleasure" in *Feminism and Sexuality: A Reader*, eds Stevie Jackson and Sue Scott (Edinburgh: Edinburgh University Press, 1996), 175–180.

James, E.L. *Fifty Shades of Grey*. New York: Vintage, 2012.

Jamieson, Lynne. *Intimacies: Personal Relationships in Modern Societies*. Cambridge: Polity Press, 1988.

Jensen, Robert. *Getting Off: Pornography and the End of Masculinity*. Cambridge, MA: South End Press, 2007.

Johnson, Merri Lisa. "Fuck You and Your Untouchable Face: Third Wave Feminism and the Problem of Romance" in *Jane Sexes It Up: True Confessions of Feminist Desire*, ed. Merri Lisa Johnson (New York: Four Walls Eight Windows, 2002), 13–50.

Johnson, Merri Lisa. "Jane Hocus, Jane Focus" in *Jane Sexes It Up: True Confessions of Feminist Desire*, ed. Merri Lisa Johnson (New York: Four Walls Eight Windows, 2002), 1–12.

Kinnick, Katherine N. "Pushing the Envelope: The Role of the Mass Media in the Mainstreaming of Pornography" in *Pop-Porn: Pornography in American Culture*, eds M.J. Bishop and A.C. Hall (Westport, CT: Praeger Publishers, 2007), 7–26.

Kneen, Krissy. *Affection: An Erotic Memoir*. Berkeley, California: Seal Press, 2010.

Lee, Abby. *Girl with a One Track Mind: Confessions of the Seductress Next Door*. London: Ebury Press, 2006.

Lewis, Sienna. *Intimate Adventures of an Office Girl*. London: Avon Books, 2009.

McLaughlin, Becky. "Sex Cuts" in *Jane Sexes It Up: True Confessions of Feminist Desire*, ed. Merri Lisa Johnson (New York: Four Walls, Eight Windows, 2002), 65–90.

DOI: 10.1057/9781137326546

McRobbie, Angela. *The Aftermath of Feminism: Gender, Culture and Social Change*. London: Sage, 2009.

Melissa P. *One Hundred Strokes of the Brush before Bed*. Translated by Lawrence Venuti. London: Serpent's Tail, 2004.

Millet, Catherine. *The Sexual Life of Catherine M*. Translated by Adriana Hunter. London: Corgi Books, 2003 [2002].

Miss S. *Confessions of a Working Girl* (London: Penguin Books, 2007).

Myers, Kathy. "Towards a Feminist Erotica" in *Sexual Lives: A Reader on the Theories and Realities of Human Sexuality*, eds Betsy Crane and Robert Heasley (New York: McGraw-Hill, 2003), 485–490.

Paasonen, Susanna. "Good Amateurs: Erotica Writing and Notions of Quality" in *Porn.com: Making Sense of Online Pornography*, ed. Feona Attwood (New York: Peter Lang, 2010), 142–158.

Porter, Dawn. *Diaries of an Internet Lover*. London: Virgin Books, 2006.

Portnoy, Suzanne. *The Butcher, the Baker, the Candlestick Maker*. London: Virgin Books, 2006.

Portnoy, Suzanne. *The Not So Invisible Woman*. London: Virgin Books, 2008.

Projansky, Sarah. *Watching Rape: Film and Television in Postfeminist Culture*. New York: New York University Press, 2001.

Quan, Tracy. *Diary of a Manhattan Call Girl*. London: Harper Perennial, 2005 [2001].

Quan, Tracy. *Diary of a Married Call Girl*. London: Harper Perennial, 2006 [2005].

Richardson, Diane. "Constructing Lesbian Identities" in *Feminism and Sexuality: A Reader*, eds Stevi Jackson and Sue Scott (Edinburgh: Edinburgh University Press, 1996), 276–286.

Rubin, Gayle. "Thinking Sex: Notes for a Radical Theory of the Politics of Sexuality" in *Pleasure and Danger: Exploring Female Sexuality*, ed. Carol Vance (London: Pandora Press, 1989), 267–319.

Sanders, Teela. *Paying for Pleasure: Men Who Buy Sex*. Portland, OR: Willan Publishing, 2008.

Segal, Lynne. *Is the Future Female?: Trouble Thoughts on Contemporary Feminism*. London: Virago, 1987.

Segal, Lynne. *Straight Sex: The Politics of Pleasure*. London: Virago, 1994.

Siegel, Deborah. *Sisterhood, Interrupted: From Radical Women to Grrrls Gone Wild*. Basingstoke: Palgrave Macmillan, 2007.

Smith, Caroline. *Cosmopolitan Culture and Consumerism in Chick Lit*. London and New York: Routledge, 2008.

Smith, Clarissa. *One for the Girls!: The Pleasures and Practices of Reading Women's Porn*. Bristol: Intellect Books, 2007.

DOI: 10.1057/9781137326546

Smith, Clarissa. "Pleasing Intensities: Masochism and Affective Pleasure in Porn Short Fictions" in *Mainstreaming Sex: The Sexualization of Western Culture*, ed. Fiona Attwood (London: I.B. Tauris, 2009), 19–36.

Tasker, Yvonne. "*Enchanted* (2007) by Postfeminism: Gender, Irony and the New Romantic Comedy" in *Feminism at the Movies: Understanding Gender in Contemporary Popular Cinema*, eds Hilary Radner and Rebecca Stringer (London and New York: Routledge, 2011).

Townsend, Catherine. *Sleeping Around: Secrets of a Sexual Adventuress.* London: John Murray, 2007.

Townsend, Catherine. *Breaking the Rules: Confessions of a Bad Girl.* London: John Murray, 2008.

Valverde, Mariana. "Pornography: Not for Men Only" in *Sexual Lives: A Reader on the Theories and Realities of Human Sexualities*, eds Betsy Crane and Robert Heasley (New York: McGraw-Hill, 2003), 467–476.

Vance, Carol. "Pleasure and Danger: Towards a Politics of Sexuality" in *Pleasure and Danger: Exploring Female Sexuality*, ed. Carol Vance (London: Pandora Press, 1989), 1–27.

Walter, Natasha. *The New Feminism.* London: Virago, 1999.

Walter, Natasha. *Living Dolls: The Return of Sexism.* London: Virago, 2010.

Warner, Michael. *The Trouble with Normal: Sex, Politics and the Ethics of Queer Life.* Cambridge, MA: Harvard University Press, 2000 [1999].

Weeks, Jeffrey. *Invented Moralities: Sexual Values in an Age of Uncertainty.* New York: Columbia University Press, 1995.

Weeks, Jeffrey. *Sexuality.* London and New York: Routledge, 2003.

Whelehan, Imelda. *Overloaded: Popular Culture and the Future of Feminism.* London: The Women's Press, 2000.

Whelehan, Imelda. *The Feminist Bestseller.* Basingstoke: Palgrave Macmillan, 2005.

Williams, Linda. *Hard Core: Power, Pleasure and the "Frenzy of the Visible".* London: Pandora Press, 1991.

Wilson-Kovacs, Dana. "Some Texts Do It Better: Women, Sexually Explicit Texts and the Everyday" in *Mainstreaming Sex: The Sexualisation of Western Cultures*, ed. Feona Attwood (London: I.B. Tauris, 2009), 137–148.

Wolf, Naomi. *Promiscuities: A Secret History of Female Desire.* London: Vintage, 1998.

Young, Mallory and Suzanne Ferriss. *Chick Lit: The New Woman's Fiction.* London and New York: Routledge, 2005.

DOI: 10.1057/9781137326546

Index

DOI: 10.1057/9781137326546

DOI: 10.1057/9781137326546

The manufacturer's authorised representative in the EU is Springer
Nature Customer Service Centre GmbH, Europaplatz 3, 69115 Heidelberg,
Germany. If you have any concerns regarding our products, please
contact ProductSafety@springernature.com

Printed and bound by CPI Group (UK) Ltd, Croydon, CR0 4YY

30/04/2026

02100171-0001